THE GIFT

Barbara Larriva

Authors Choice Press
San Jose New York Lincoln Shanghai

The Gift

Authors Choice Press
an imprint of iUniverse.com, Inc.

For information address:
iUniverse.com, Inc.
5220 S 16th, Ste. 200
Lincoln, NE 68512
www.iuniverse.com

Originally published by Ballantine Books

ISBN: 0-595-17786-7

Printed in the United States of America

For my son . . .
Gregory Jude Larriva
. . . with love.

Chapter One

Hands on her hips, Dove Anderson surveyed the chaos of dirty dishes and used utensils spread over the counters. The Mexican-tiled kitchen was usually neat and orderly, but today was an exception to that rule. With a shrug, she tucked her auburn hair behind her ears and headed toward the refrigerator.

As she passed the window, she caught a glimpse of her daughter Donna splashing in the pool with her friends, and two-year-old Robby in his new blue sunsuit, playing in the sandbox. She quickened her steps; she would have to hurry if she wanted to whip the kitchen into shape and make the potato salad before her sister and other guests arrived. And the cake had to be iced too, she reminded herself, blowing an errant strand of hair off her forehead as she hastened back to the sink.

A few minutes later, Donna poked her head in the doorway, a small puddle forming at her feet. "Why are you crying, Mom?"

"It's this onion," Dove sniffled, dabbing at her eyes. She reached for the beach towel draped over a kitchen chair and tossed it to her daughter. "How's my birthday girl? Having fun?"

"Yes, but . . ." Donna hesitated, droplets of water cling-

1

ing to long eyelashes that shaded her brown eyes. "Can we call Doctor Franklin and ask him to bring over some of the kids from the Deaf and Blind School? They probably never get to go to parties."

"What a thoughtful idea, Donna. I'm sure they'd love to come. But you'd better make the call. I'm up to my elbows in onions and mayonnaise."

Donna laughed. "Sure." Minutes later she was back in the kitchen, yanking the telephone wire behind her. "Doctor Franklin said he could be here with the kids in about a half hour. He wants to talk to you first."

Rinsing off her hands, Dove said over her shoulder, "Dad and I will be out in a little bit. Okay?"

"Sure, Mom. I'm going back in the pool."

"Don't forget to keep the pool gate closed," Dove called after Donna as she balanced the phone between her shoulder and ear. "Hi, Doctor Franklin. No, no, it won't be any trouble at all. I think it will be great for the kids. It was totally Donna's idea so don't worry about ruining her party. Good. See you soon."

"Who's going to ruin the party?" Bob asked, coming behind Dove and putting his arms around his wife.

She turned into his embrace. "Nobody, silly. You know we don't allow parties to be ruined around here." Looking up at him, she said, "Have you noticed Donna has a special glow about her today?"

"That's because it's her birthday." Bob led Dove into the living room, away from the demands of the kitchen.

"I guess." Then turning to Bob, she said, "You know what she just did? She called Doctor Franklin and asked him to bring some of the children over."

"It doesn't surprise me. Donna has always been very outgoing and giving."

"Yes, but it's her birthday. I would have thought she'd just want to have fun with her friends."

"She'll do that, too. She's good at doing two things at once."

Smiling, Dove said, "She's a lot more mature than I was at fifteen."

Bob pulled Dove to his side. "You weren't so bad—if I can remember that far back. . . ."

"Oh, you," she laughed, hitting him with one of the small pillows from the sofa.

Bob grabbed Dove and wrapped her in a bear hug, swinging her around. "Deep down inside you haven't changed much. You're still the same gangly redhead I fell in love with on the beach."

"And you're still the handsome, gentle, kind person you were then."

Dove had loved Bob from the day she'd met him on Catalina Island. Her mother had thought it was puppy love, but Dove had known better, even then. It was Bob who helped her through that terrible year when she was engulfed in feelings of guilt. How could she not love him? He was everything she'd ever wanted.

As she looked up at him, she thought he was even more handsome now with his sun-streaked blond hair and dark blue eyes.

As of one mind they both sat on the sofa, and Dove took Bob's hand. "We've made all our dreams come true, haven't we, Bob?—your schoolboy dream of becoming a minister and my dream of being your wife and the mother of your children. And I mustn't forget my kids from the Deaf and Blind School."

Bob nodded thoughtfully. "God has been extremely good to us. He's blessed us with an abundance of love and happiness."

"I know. Sometimes it scares me. . . ."

Bob took Dove's face in his hands. "Don't be afraid. It's His wish that all His children are happy."

She nodded. "I've come a long way since we met. You've taught me so much—so very much."

Bob hugged her. "Hey, I thought this was supposed to be a party! That kitchen looked like a cyclone hit it. Need any help?"

"I thought you'd never ask," she said as they stood and walked toward the kitchen.

Dove went back to mixing the potato salad while Bob poured grape juice and seltzer water into the punch bowl. The screen door slammed, and Dove looked up as Donna and Robby came in.

"He's thirsty," Donna said, heading for the refrigerator to get ice.

"Hey, sport," Bob said, picking up the toddler. "What've you been up to? Having fun at your sister's party?"

Robby wriggled to get down. "Thirsty," he said, pointing to the fruit punch. Reluctantly Bob released him.

"Want some, Mom? Dad?" Donna handed a small plastic glass to Robby, who quickly drained it.

They shook their heads. "Not for me," Bob said, munching on a potato chip. "Tell me, daughter-of-mine, how does it feel to be fifteen? Any different today than yesterday?"

"Oh, Dad, don't tease. You know there's no difference."

He ruffled her damp hair. "You look prettier."

Dove smiled as she watched Donna's cheeks redden. Then Donna quickly recovered and said, "That's because I have such good-looking parents."

"Touché," Dove said.

"When are you guys going to be finished in here so you can come out with us?" Donna asked.

"By the time Aunt Maddy gets here, I'll be finished. Then we'll all come outside."

"Gotcha," Bob said, carrying Robby outside, with Donna following close on his heels.

Dove covered the large bowl of potato salad with plastic wrap and put it in the refrigerator. After straightening up the kitchen, she walked to the window and pushed the yellow- and -white dotted swiss curtain back. With love in her eyes, she watched Robby trying to maneuver his tricycle. Then she turned her attention to Donna and watched her dive into the pool and surface. Donna's face brightened when she saw her mother in the window and she waved to her. Smiling, Dove waved back.

Every day she reminds me more and more of Maddy, Dove thought, remembering Donna's call to Doctor Franklin. They both have that special sensitivity.

She closed her eyes, and the memory of another fifteenth birthday unfolded. Hers and Maddy's. Maddy, her twin sister, Madonna.

Chapter Two

Dove struggled to get the comb through her tangled red hair and wound up throwing the black piece of plastic across her bedroom in frustration. "Why did I inherit all the bad traits and you all the good ones? I thought twins were supposed to be the same," she complained for the hundredth time to her sister, Maddy.

"Oh come on, Dove, you play that broken record all the time. You know you don't have all the bad traits, and I certainly don't have all the good ones. What's wrong with your flaming red hair?" Maddy teased as she sat down on Dove's bed.

"It's ugly! That's what's wrong with it. But look at you—long, straight, shiny black hair. Big brown eyes that let you get away with murder. Then to top it off, you're short, with little hands and feet. . . ."

"I know, I know. Your hair is kinky, your eyes are watered-down blue, you're a giant with elephant feet. . . ." She started to giggle. "Really Dove, you're a freak."

"You got that right! And don't forget the freckles. I'm surprised I'm not cross-eyed, too," Dove grumbled, crossing her eyes hideously as she turned back to the mirror. Trying to ignore her twin's laugh, she looked at her sister reflected in the glass and once again felt the stab of jealousy. It wasn't fair. Maddy had it all. She got the dregs.

Suddenly angry, Dove spun around. "It's okay for you to laugh," she lashed out. "I'm the one who wears a size eight shoe and has hands like King Kong."

"Come off it, Dove. Your fingers are long and graceful."

Dove drew in a deep, despairing sigh. "But don't you see, Maddy? I don't want long and graceful fingers. I don't want red hair. I don't want to be a head taller than everyone else in school—especially the boys. I just want to be normal. Small. Pretty. Ordinary. Why couldn't we have been *identical* twins? I'd give anything to look like you." With a groan of defeat, Dove threw herself down on the bed next to Maddy.

"There's nothing wrong with the way you look—you're—you're distinctive," Maddy said and put her arm around her sister. "And you want to know something? I've always wished my hair was the color of yours."

Dove looked at her in disbelief. "You have?"

Maddy took one of Dove's red curls and let it twine around her finger. "Like a shiny copper penny. Mine's just plain ordinary black—and poker straight."

"Oh, you're just saying that to make me feel good." Dove bit down on her bottom lip, holding back the tears. She was never afraid to be herself in front of Maddy or to say what was on her mind because Maddy was more than a sister—she was her best friend. They were particularly close when school was out because most of their friends spent the summer on the mainland, although Maddy had a new boyfriend, a senior named Allen. Maddy said he was *just a friend*, but to Dove it was all the same thing. He was a boy. Dove sighed to herself, wondering if she was ever going to have a boyfriend. The prospects didn't look too good. What guy in his right mind would want a redheaded giant for a girlfriend?

"Come on, Dove," Maddy said, breaking into her thoughts. "You know I don't just say things to make people feel good. Especially you."

"I know." Dove looked at her sister, affection shining from her pale blue eyes. "But still . . ." Dove wanted to believe that Maddy was right—that she wasn't weird-looking—but her feelings about herself crowded out Maddy's words. "And another thing. It's not easy going around with a name like Dove," she continued. "All the kids at school call me Bird Legs." She stuck her long legs out in front of her and studied them. "But you know something? I think they're right." She burst into giggles and stretched out on the pink bedspread, her legs dangling over the edge.

"One of these days people will refer to you as 'that tall, willowy redhead with the pearly blue eyes.' "

Dove promptly threw a pillow at her sister. "You got that line from Mom."

"Well, it's true."

"Hmmm, but can I wait that long?" Leaning on her elbow, Dove asked thoughtfully, "Where do you think Mom ever came up with such dumb names? Maddy's not a bad nickname—but *Madonna*! That's almost as bad as Dove."

"She probably confiscated them from some books she liked."

"Confiscated?" Dove wrinkled her nose.

Maddy shrugged nonchalantly. "You know, took . . . borrowed . . ."

"Well, wherever she got them, they're weird!" She reached out and touched Maddy's long, silky hair. "But you want to know something? Madonna kind of fits you. You really do look like the Madonnas I studied in art history last year. They all had long black hair and big round brown eyes."

"That's because they were Italian."

Dove shrugged away Maddy's comment and then shook her head. "Well, as dumb as our names are, I guess we're stuck with them. But when I have a kid she's going to have a common name like Pat or Joan or maybe even Mary."

"How about Robin?" Maddy teased.

"No birds!" Dove shrieked and threw the other pillow at her sister.

"What's all that commotion up there?" Ann Sanders called from downstairs. "And what's taking you girls so long to get changed? Get a move on. We're going to be eating pretty soon."

Dove made a wry face and Maddy called out, "We'll be right down, Mom."

Dove went to her closet while Maddy studied her reflection in front of the long mirror.

"Want me to fix up your eyes like Cleopatra's later on?" Maddy asked eagerly.

"Ugh. My eyes are bad enough without putting that gloppy stuff on them. And besides, Mom would kill us if she found out."

"It's not like we're going to go into town or anything. I just thought it would be fun to try here in the house," Maddy said.

"That junk's not for me." Dismissing the idea, Dove asked, "What're you going to wear?"

"My yellow dress. See you downstairs. Don't take too long or Mom'll get mad." She walked down the hall to her room.

Dove stared for a long moment at the clothes hanging haphazardly in her closet. She didn't like dresses. They made her feel all arms and legs. But her mother preferred them, so Dove reluctantly pulled out a turquoise dress. "At least this color makes my eyes look darker," she told her reflection. With a sigh she held up the dress in front of her, nodding approval to her image in the mirror. "It'll have to do," she muttered.

After she was dressed, Dove combed over the top layer of her wavy copper hair, figuring nobody would see underneath anyhow. She rummaged through her dresser to find Maddy's birthday present that she had hidden weeks ago. It's perfect for her, Dove thought as she shoved the drawer closed and ran down the stairs two at a time.

"Can't you ever walk?" Her mother asked the same old

question from the dining room as she took the dishes from the sideboard.

"My legs are too long to take the stairs one at a time," came Dove's usual answer.

"Oh, for heaven's sake." Her mother laughed lightly. "You make it sound like you're a giant. You're only five-six."

"*Only?* By the time I'm eighteen I'll probably be six feet tall."

"Don't exaggerate, Dove. Most likely you'll grow another inch or two and then stop."

Dove studied her petite, dark-haired mother. "That's easy for you to say. You don't have to worry about growing anymore." Then she glanced around. "Where's Dad and Maddy?"

"They're both in the backyard. I'm glad you're wearing a dress, because we're going to church tonight."

"Church?" Dove groaned, wrinkling her nose. "Why church? On our birthday? Can't we go to the movies?"

"The Little Church on the Hill is having its first healing service tonight at seven, and I thought we should go as part of the community."

"Oh, yuk! Nobody in this family needs any healing." Dove dropped Maddy's present on the lacy white tablecloth that covered the antique oval table, then pushed the perfectly wrapped box next to Maddy's plate. It had cost her an extra fifty cents to have the present gift-wrapped. Suddenly, she spun around to her mother, a worried look in her eyes. "You're not sick are you?"

"No, no. I just want to see what the service is like. I understand they'll be having one every Tuesday night." A teasing grin flashed across her round face. "Won't hurt you two to attend. Besides, I think you'll find it interesting."

"Looks like we don't have any choice." She shrugged, then announced, "I'm going out to get Maddy and Dad."

"Tell them dinner's ready, will you?"

Slamming the screen door behind her, Dove ran across the small lawn.

Ann Sanders shook her head and watched her daughter trample the grass and jump over the flower beds. It never failed to amaze her how two sisters could be so different—not only in looks but in temperament. Maddy rarely raised her voice, but Dove wouldn't hesitate to screech if her temper called for it. The fact that they were twins made it even harder for her to understand. Dove definitely had her father's coloring, though his rusty hair was straight. I guess she got her curls from me, Ann thought, running her fingers through her own black curls. And she's tall like her dad.

But does that girl ever complain! She's forever bemoaning the color of her eyes. They're truly unique—sometimes soft as Wedgwood blue, yet other times, when she's quiet and deep in concentration, they look like blue pearls. Ann laughed aloud; she had never seen a blue pearl. Turning from the screen door, she walked into the sunny kitchen, grabbed two pot holders, and removed the chicken from the oven.

Dove poked her head into the doorway of the shed. "What are you hiding?" she asked as Maddy looked up and hastily shoved a box into her father's arms.

"Don't look!" Maddy's face mirrored the excitement of a secret. "It's your birthday present. I wasn't going to give it to you till after we ate."

Consumed with curiosity, Dove moved closer to her father and tried to peek into the box.

"Hold on, let me get it for you." Maddy slipped past her and reached into the box. She dropped a ball of white fur into Dove's outstretched hands and waited.

"Oh, Maddy. A white kitten!" Rubbing the soft fur against her face, she exclaimed, "Listen to it purr. Oh, thank you, I love it. It's adorable!" Giving her sister a quick kiss, she asked, "Is it a girl?" Maddy nodded. Turning the kitten over, Dove began to laugh.

"What's so funny. Does she have six toes?" Maddy asked.

"There's nothing wrong with her toes, but did you get a

look at her eyes? They're blue, poor thing." Still laughing, she continued, "Not just ordinary blue, but . . ."

"I know. I know. Spare me. Watered down blue exactly like yours. Right?" Maddy finished, joining her sister in laughter.

"You got it. And I have the perfect name for her—Paloma—it means 'dove' in Spanish." When their laughter died down to a chuckle, Dove asked, "Has Mom seen her?"

A huge grin spread across Joe Sanders's face. "Not yet. Why don't you go in and show her."

"Do you think she'll like Paloma?" Dove asked.

"She'll love her," Maddy answered. "When Dad and I were choosing her, he told me he and Mom used to have a cat a long time ago." She glanced over her shoulder to their father, who was walking behind them.

"It must have been long ago. I don't remember any cats." When they reached the back porch, Dove stopped and said eagerly, "I hope you like your present as much as I like Paloma."

"Oh, Dove, I've loved everything you've ever given me."

"Even that terrible crocheted hanky I made?"

"Even that."

They burst into peals of laughter at the memory of the white piece of cloth bordered in uneven loops of red and orange yarn. In the kitchen, Dove held up the tiny fluff of fur for her mother's inspection. "Mom, *look*. A kitten!"

A slight frown creased Ann's forehead. "Nobody checked with me before bringing a kitten into the house."

"I asked Dad," Maddy answered, looking at her father for confirmation. "He said it would be okay."

Ann wiped her hands on her apron. "Here. Let me hold her," she said, reaching out for the kitten. She noticed Joe watching her, a tender smile softening the rugged lines of his face, and she knew that he too was remembering the kitten they'd found on their honeymoon.

Ann and Joe had married right after graduating from

high school in Los Angeles. After pooling their meager savings, they found they had only enough money to get to Catalina for their honeymoon.

Starry-eyed, they took the boat to the village of Avalon and their love for each other reached out to encompass the quaint, magical island off the California coast. On their first night on Catalina, they vowed to live on the island when Joe finished college.

On the way to Pebbly Beach the next day, they'd come across a gaunt gray and white striped kitten, and their hearts immediately went out to the little creature. They'd continued walking to the beach but stayed less than an hour, both of them worrying about the stray kitten. Ann remembered how relieved she'd been when Joe suggested they retrace their steps to try to find it. The tiny animal seemed to be waiting for them. Ann picked him up carefully, carried him back to the hotel, and put a little milk in an ashtray. They named him Jake, hid him from the hotel maids, and made plans to smuggle him back to the mainland. Ann had a wicker basket and poked extra holes in it for air. Four years later, when they returned to Catalina to live permanently, Jake made the passage in a well-ventilated kennel.

Ann smiled, remembering, and then looked down at the fluffy white kitten in her hand. When Jake died twelve years ago, she'd sworn she'd have no more pets in the house, but holding Paloma erased that long-ago promise.

Dove saw her mother smile and cuddle Paloma against her cheek; the kitten was here to stay. Dragging Maddy by the hand, she led her into the dining room. "Here's your present," she said, handing Maddy her carefully wrapped gift. Dove wasn't disappointed when Maddy's eyes opened wide.

"A gold I.D. bracelet! Oh, Dove, what a super present."

"It's not real gold," Dove said sheepishly.

"It is to me." Maddy hugged her sister tightly and whispered in her ear, "I'm never going to take it off."

"You will if it turns your arm green," she said flippantly, but deep inside Dove beamed at her sister's reaction.

"It won't. It's going to stay shiny gold forever. You'll see. Put it on for me, will you?" Maddy held out her left arm, and Dove fastened the clasp and watched proudly as Maddy spun around, showing off her new bracelet.

"Come," Ann said, glancing conspiratorially at Joe, "there's still more. So how about everybody washing up for dinner. Dove, first take the kitten up to your room. I hope somebody thought about litter and food." Ann looked questioningly from Maddy to Joe.

"It's in my room," Maddy answered. "I hid everything in the closet."

"Be right back," Dove called as she ran up the stairs, still stroking the kitten. She set up the litter box, then crooned to the kitten. "Oh, Paloma, I'm so glad you're mine." She turned the kitten around to look at its eyes again. "Poor thing," she murmured, giggling, and placed the kitten on her pink and white pillow before closing the door behind her.

"Hurry, Dove," Maddy said, as her twin entered the dining room. Two small boxes, identically wrapped, lay in front of the girls' plates. They hastily tore off the wrapping paper, opening the boxes at the same time.

"Pierced earrings!" Maddy exclaimed, holding up tiny gold seashells. "Oh, Mom, you finally gave in. When can we get our ears pierced?"

Before Ann could answer, Dove said rapidly. "Janie's mother pierces ears all the time. If I call and she says yes can we go after dinner? Can we, Mom? Can we?"

"We're going to church, remember?" Ann said.

Both girls groaned, then Dove brightened. "We could go on the way. It won't take long. Janie said it only takes about five minutes. Please, Mom."

"Call and ask. Then we'd better get on with dinner or we'll run out of time."

One of the things Dove loved about living on Catalina Island was that Avalon was so small. Everything was within walking distance or at most, five minutes away by car. And it was safe to walk around. Sometimes her dad would drive her and Maddy to Front Street—Crescent Avenue to the tourists—and pick them up a couple of hours later. It was like being on vacation year round.

Sure, she had to go to school, but she didn't have to spend too much time studying. Neither did Maddy. School was easy for both of them. Their outside interests differed though. Dove loved to snorkel and swim, and it was beyond her how Maddy could stay in the house reading for hours at a time. Dove read what was required in school and not another word. Maddy was also interested in stained glass. She kept her supplies in a corner of the shed their father had set aside for her. Dove had tried it once, but she broke more glass than what was needed for the pattern she was working on. Defeated, she decided her hands were too big to handle the small pieces.

After they sang happy birthday, Ann cut into the white frosted cake with blue sailboats. Dove asked for the end piece, thick with icing, while Maddy asked for a much smaller piece.

"One of the advantages of being tall and thin," Maddy sighed as she watched Dove eat. When they finished their cake and ice cream, Joe casually said, "Before you three take off for church, I have something for Dove and Maddy. Follow me." The girls trailed their father out the back door and behind the shed. Propped against it were two ten-speed bicycles. One was blue, the other silver. "Take your pick," he said, beaming.

"Gosh, I don't know which one I like best. Which one do you like, Maddy?" Dove said with her fingers crossed behind her back.

"Well, the silver's a little too flashy for me. . . ."

Before Maddy had a chance to reconsider, Dove said, "I'll take it!" and walked over to the shiny bike.

"Maddy, that okay with you?" questioned her father.

"Oh, yes. I like the blue one better." She ran her hand over the smooth metal.

"Good. I'll get the baskets on for you in the morning before I go to work. How's that?"

The girls ran to their father and hugged him. "Great! Thanks, Dad. I can't wait to try it out," Dove bubbled, thinking of the freedom she'd now have to roam the island.

"Me, too." Suddenly Maddy grabbed Dove's arm. "What's all this about going to church tonight?"

"Oh, there's some weird healing service. Mom wants to go, and she said we have to go too."

"Dove," her father said in a reprimanding tone.

"Are you going, Dad?" Maddy asked.

"Afraid I can't. We're short one man at the hotel, and I told them I'd stop by after dinner to help out." He put his arms around his daughters, and they walked back to the house.

Now that Dove knew she was getting her ears pierced, going to church didn't seem all that awful. She was glad she'd put on a dress. She never would have thought that the combination of being dressed up and having pierced ears could make her feel so grown up, but it did.

Janie was waiting for them at the door. The chubby, blond girl seemed as eager as the twins and ushered them into the kitchen, where her mother waited. Sue Proctor was an older version of her daughter.

"Want some coffee?" Sue asked Ann.

"No thanks. We've just had dinner."

Janie set out the cotton and alcohol while her mother scrubbed her hands.

It didn't hurt much. Just a little prick in each ear and it was over. Dove held up the mirror Janie handed her and admired her new earrings. She pushed her hair behind her ears to better show them off. Maddy quickly braided her black hair into one long braid that hung over her right shoulder, then hugged her mother. "Thanks again, Mom," she said, reaching up to touch one of the seashells.

They thanked Janie's mother and listened to the simple instructions about how to care for their ears, then left for church. "What is a healing service, Mom?" Dove asked as they walked up Clarissa Street. "Isn't it kind of scary?"

"Of course it isn't scary. The minister just focuses on someone who needs healing and prays over that person. Sometimes the congregation prays as a group. At least that's what I was told. I learned about healing services years ago, before your Dad and I moved to Catalina. When I was working as a waitress to help put him through college, one of the other waitresses complained that her back used to bother her because she was on her feet so much. She said she got rid of the pain that way."

"She did?" Maddy asked, and her mother nodded as they crossed the street and stood before the white stucco church.

Dove noticed Maddy's instant interest. Maddy went in for things like that, but to Dove it was just scary. Suddenly she shuddered.

The Little Church on the Hill was fairly new and not very large. The girls had been attending Sunday services for about a year, but this was their first healing service. As they walked up the steps, Dove cast a furtive glance at her sister, but Maddy appeared serene. For some reason Dove felt anxious—perhaps because she didn't know what to expect and because it sounded so *religious*. Dove believed in God and said her prayers at night when she remembered, but that was the extent of her faith. And then, quite unexpectedly, the palms of her hands began to perspire.

Ann led them down the center aisle to an empty pew. When they were seated, Dove nervously touched her ears to cover the feeling of anxiety building inside her. She glanced over at Maddy, but she had picked up a pamphlet and was leafing through it. Unable to quell her mounting anxiety, Dove gazed around the church. The oak pews were shiny, as if someone had just polished them. It was a plain church, but the stained glass windows made it beautiful. Dove loved to watch the colors come to life when the bright morning sun shone through them. They looked different now.

Someone coughed, and Dove's attention turned to the congregation. It wasn't very crowded tonight, maybe fifteen or twenty people. She didn't recognize any of them. Most were old—older than her mother. They all seemed so *holy*, with their heads bowed in prayer, their lips moving noiselessly. What a bunch of weird people, she thought.

Dove squirmed in her seat. She wished the service would hurry up and start so it would hurry up and end and she could hurry up and go home. She wanted to play with Paloma and to look at her new earrings in the mirror.

Reverend Franklin O. Honeycutt lumbered to the pulpit. He was a large, robust man in his early fifties with thinning blond hair. Dove knew him to be a soft-spoken, gentle person. Just as he was about to begin the service, Dove made room beside herself for an elderly white-haired woman.

Reverend Honeycutt opened the Bible, cleared his throat, and began speaking. "Tonight I will read from Matthew about prayer and forgiveness. Remember, my dear friends in Christ, we cannot be healed if we harbor resentment or hate against anyone."

He picked up the Holy Book and began reading: " 'I tell you solemnly once again, if two of you on earth agree to ask anything at all, it will be granted to you by my Father in heaven. For when two or three meet in my name, I shall be there with them.' "

Dove's mind wandered. She stared at the pale gray carpet covered with splashes of gold and amethyst, rose and jade from the waning evening sun shining through the stained glass. She wondered if Maddy would make church windows someday.

The minister's words droned on and on, and then the sudden quiet in the church brought Dove back to her surroundings.

From the rear of the church, a man began speaking, and the strange words caught Dove's attention.

"My children, someone in this church is in great physical pain, but never complains. Instead, the suffering is offered to me daily as a sacrifice of love. Tonight, my children, that person's silent prayer will be answered."

Dove fought the urge to turn around to see who was talking. Ann sensed her curiosity; she turned to Dove and whispered, "It's the gift of prophecy. The Lord is speaking through him."

The calm voice of a woman called out from the pew behind Dove, "I felt the Lord saying the same thing."

And then it was a jumble of "Praise the Lord," "Alleluia," and "Thank you, Jesus."

Dove heard Reverend Honeycutt say, " 'And these signs shall follow all who believe, they shall lay their hands upon the sick, who will recover.' Now let's all stand, hold hands, and sing the Lord's Prayer." Maddy and Ann stood up; Dove reluctantly followed their lead.

Glancing down at the old woman's gnarled hand, Dove shuddered at the thought of having to hold it. She thought about changing places with Maddy, but was afraid she'd cause a scene and that was the last thing she wanted to do. Taking a deep breath to fortify herself, she folded her long slender fingers over the woman's deformed hand. Maddy smiled at Dove as the strains of the organ filled the church, and Dove managed a weak smile in return.

Suddenly, Dove's feeling of anxiety overwhelmed her. Something strange was happening. She didn't know exactly what it was, but she could sense it. Maddy had intuitions like this all the time; she could help her, Dove thought frantically. But it was too late. The hymn had already begun.

"*Our Father, who art in heaven, hallowed be thy name.*" A wave of heat rushed through Dove and seemed to settle in her hands. "*Thy kingdom come, thy will be done on earth as it is in heaven.*" Her hands began to tingle as if they were on fire. "*Give us this day our daily bread and forgive us our trespasses as we forgive those who trespass against us.*" She wanted to flee the small church and had to force herself to stay. "*And lead us not into temptation, but deliver us from evil.*" Dove thought she was going to faint. *"For thine is the kingdom, and the power, and the glory forever and ever. Amen."*

When the hymn was finally over, Dove dropped the woman's hand and sank onto the pew, trying to sort out her feelings. Why was she so scared? And why had she felt faint a moment ago? She'd never fainted in her life. Suddenly, with no warning, her confusion vanished, replaced by the most beautiful peacefulness. She looked around. A lovely calm seemed to envelop the tiny church. She'd never noticed it before. But then she'd never felt like this before either.

Suddenly a scream from the old woman sitting next to her shattered the silence. Dove's heart skipped a beat, then pounded furiously in her chest. She glanced around in panic. Mom was wrong. This service *was* scary!

"My hand! Look at my hand!" the woman shouted, waving it in the air.

The entire congregation turned to look at the hand that moments before had been gnarled and twisted. Now it was smooth and straight. "I'm healed, I'm healed," she shouted and stood up.

"Praise the Lord!" someone called out reverently.

"I knew something was happening when she took my hand," the old woman said, pointing to Dove. "I felt this—this heat come out of Dove's hand and go into mine. She's a healer, I tell you. She's a healer." She began sobbing almost hysterically, repeating over and over again, "God be praised—I'm healed—the Lord worked His miracle through this young girl."

Every eye in the church turned from the old woman to stare in astonishment at Dove, who cringed in her seat, pressing against Maddy.

"She's crazy," she whispered, frantically wanting to run, an uneasy feeling washing over her, as if she'd gotten caught doing something she wasn't supposed to do. But she hadn't done anything tonight.

The congregation began talking excitedly, some kneeling in prayer, others waving their hands as they chanted,

"Praise God," or "Amen." Then suddenly, as though directed by some unseen hand, they rose and began moving toward Dove and the old woman. Though they numbered fewer than twenty, they seemed like a crazed mob to Dove. She moaned softly as spots swam before her eyes until she felt blackness washing over her.

The last thing she remembered was whispering voices praising the Lord.

Chapter Three

Her heart pounding, Ann Sanders quickly changed places with Maddy and held Dove against her shoulder. Looking around the pew, she found a pamphlet and began fanning her daughter's face with it.

"Please. Everyone, get back," she ordered in a tight voice. "She needs air." In unison, as if rehearsed, the small congregation moved back a step. They continued staring in awe, first at the old woman's hand and then at Dove's pale face.

The woman was no stranger to the Little Church on the Hill. Ann knew Genevieve Farley; they had both served on the Adopt-a-Family Committee the previous Christmas. She remembered how Genevieve's arthritically crippled hand had encumbered her work. Now, she cast a furtive glance at that hand. She could see that something *had* straightened it.

Ann clutched Dove closer as if to protect her, but from what she didn't know.

Reverend Honeycutt came down the aisle, and the small crowd parted to let him through. He looked down at Dove's peaceful face—as still as if carved in stone—and then lifted Genevieve's extended hand. "Praise the Lord," he breathed. "We've seen a miracle."

"Praise God," a voice called out, and several *amens* sounded in answer.

Suddenly the crowd came to life again, and people began shoving their way toward Genevieve Farley, looking from her straightened hand to Dove's serene face.

"Genevieve!" a woman called from the back of the crowd. "You say you felt heat coming from the girl's hand?"

"Oh, there was heat all right. And you can see for yourself the result." She offered her hand excitedly.

A young woman in front fell to her knees and began sobbing. An elderly couple helped her to her feet and comforted the emotional woman.

Dove opened her eyes for a moment and glanced around her. Leaning further into her mother's shoulder, she closed them again.

Charlie Hale, a pathetically thin old man, squeezed through the group of people hovering around Mrs. Farley. "Please let me touch the girl," he begged, his long, bony fingers reaching out to Dove.

Reverend Honeycutt stepped in front of him and said gently, "Charlie, the child has fainted—she needs air." He looked at the parishioners inching forward. "Please. Everyone move back a little. We must remain calm or we'll frighten the child when she comes to."

Undaunted, the man tried again to touch Dove and exclaimed, "An angel of the Lord, that's what she is." His eyes became unusually bright as he turned to face the crowd and announced solemnly, "As God is my witness, I *know* she can cure my emphysema."

Reverend Honeycutt took Charlie by the arm and guided him to a pew on the other side of the church, assuring him he would take him to Dove when she was fully recovered. More people began shoving closer to Dove. "Let me see her," an elderly man said as he pushed his way through. "She does look angelic."

The minister's voice rose above the babble. "Please, please, friends." He wiped his brow and then shoved the white cloth back into his pocket. He looked around the small church, hoping everything was under control. When his gaze rested, it was on Dove.

Suddenly Ann was frightened. Genevieve Farley seemed to have been forgotten, and Dove was now the focus of everyone's attention. She knew her daughter had nothing to do with the healing. But how was she to convince them? Ann felt claustrophobic in the small church.

Maddy leaned toward her mother and whispered, "Is Dove okay?"

Ann nodded, looking down at her daughter's peaceful face. "She came to a few minutes ago. I think she's fallen asleep. Probably her mind's way of shutting out a frightening experience. Go call Dad at the hotel and tell him to come right away. Wait for him outside." Maddy slipped out of the pew and into the vestibule.

"This is some kind of mistake," Ann said shakily to Reverend Honeycutt before turning to Genevieve. "My daughter couldn't possibly have had anything to do with your healing. Just because she stood next to you and held your hand doesn't mean a thing. She didn't even want to come to church tonight."

Feeling Dove move against her, Ann spoke urgently, "Look, why don't you all go home and . . . and just forget this ever happened. I don't want my daughter stared at and talked about because of a chance seating arrangement."

"Forget this ever happened!" echoed Genevieve. "Look at my hand. I can move it just like my other one. How can I forget it ever happened? You can make believe it didn't happen, Ann, but it did. And it was because of Dove. I tell you I felt it when she held my hand."

"You're crazy," Ann lashed out.

"Ladies, ladies, please," Reverend Honeycutt exclaimed. "We need to remain calm. There was obviously a miracle. But was this child responsible?" His gaze rested once more on Dove.

"Reverend Honeycutt, only God performs miracles," one of the women in the crowd interjected. Ann felt that these words were the only ones that had made any sense since Genevieve's healing.

Again he raised his hands to calm the congregation. "Of course, God is the only one who heals. But sometimes He moves in mysterious ways. Ways we do not understand. These are the times we should open ourselves to receive His blessings and rejoice in His glorious works. Let me quote a passage from John: 'Truly, truly, I say to you, he who believes in me will also do the works that I do, and greater works than these will he do because I go to the Father. Whatever you ask in my name, I will do it, that the Father may be glorified in the Son.' "

He cleared his throat and continued, "What I meant was—is this child a channel for healing? And if so, will she be able to do it again?" He looked from Ann's stricken face to Dove's, innocent in unconsciousness. Again Ann heard the murmur of several *amens*.

I have to get Dove out of here, she thought. This is witchcraft in reverse and it's crazy. They're going to try to make a saint out of her.

"Because of Dove's condition, I think we should end tonight's service. But let us first sing a hymn of praise to our loving Father," Reverend Honeycutt suggested.

The organist took his cue, and strains of "How Great Thou Art" filled the church. The voices of the people rang out with conviction that God was truly great and had performed a miracle in their small church.

Ann's heart sank as she saw some of the congregation sit down again after the hymn, their curious stares directed to the pew she and Dove occupied.

She watched a few file out of the little church, one or two pushing their way to the door, as if they couldn't wait to spread the news. Biting down on her bottom lip, she closed her eyes to block out the sight.

Dove's weak voice broke into Ann's thoughts. "Mom, what happened? Why am I leaning on you?"

"You healed . . ." Genevieve Farley began, but was stopped when Ann's hand shot out and grabbed her wrist.

"Quit saying that!" Ann said through clenched teeth.

Reverend Honeycutt leaned against the pew and spoke directly to Dove. "We had a miracle tonight," he said before Ann could stop him.

"A miracle? What miracle? What's he talking about, Mom?" Dove pulled away and tugged on her skirt in embarrassment. Her light blue eyes were luminous, and under the bewilderment her face glowed softly.

Ann's throat was so dry she was unable to answer.

"You see, my dear, you were holding Mrs. Farley's hand—the one that had been crippled with arthritis," the minister explained, leaning closer to Dove, "when we sang the Lord's Prayer. And when the hymn ended, Mrs. Farley's hand was . . . no longer crippled."

Confused by the minister's words, Dove tried to remember what Mrs. Farley's hand had looked like before. Yes . . . all knobby and ugly. She made a face. "So? This was a healing service and she was healed. Isn't that what's supposed to happen?"

His smile was upsetting to Dove and she moved back. "Mrs. Farley thinks your touch healed her." He spoke solemnly. "She said she felt . . ."

"Oh, no!" Dove said, shaking her head, suddenly afraid. "You've got it all wrong. I don't know anything about healing." Her heart began pounding, and she looked at Mrs. Farley with growing panic. Drawing back close to her mother, as though for protection, she mumbled, "I didn't even want to come here tonight. Right, Mom?" Seeing the worried expression on her mother's face scared Dove even more. "Let's get out of here," she begged.

Ann slid a protective arm around her. "Yes, dear. Maddy went to call Dad, and he should be here in a few minutes." She patted Dove's shoulder. "We're going to take you home."

A few people who had remained in the church approached them.

"Don't leave yet," a young woman begged Dove.

"Maybe there are others here you can heal. Won't you please try? Just lay your hands on us."

Dove cringed at the woman's words. She's as loony as the old people, she thought. Had the whole world suddenly gone crazy?

Mrs. Farley held out her hand again and spoke to Ann. "Ann, you can't ignore what happened. Your daughter needs to know the facts before you leave."

"Who are you to tell me what Dove needs?" Ann snapped. "I know what's best for my daughter."

"Why don't you ask me?" Dove said. "I know the facts. And the facts are that I had absolutely nothing to do with your healing."

Ann put her hand on Dove's arm to quiet her.

"Look," Mrs. Farley commanded, holding out her hand.

Dove glanced at it, and a sharp feeling of panic coursed through her. Fear invaded her senses; she did not know why and felt slightly disoriented.

"Please, please," Reverend Honeycutt said, spreading his arms out. "Again I must ask you to remember—this is a church. Let's not tarnish the miracle with bickering."

"Ann, what's going on?" Joe's voice sounded from the doorway. He hurried down the aisle, Maddy directly behind him, shoving past those crowded around his wife and daughter, and stopped at the pew.

Ann touched her husband's arm, relieved to see him. "Let's get Dove out of here, Joe," she said tightly. "This church has turned into a madhouse." His questioning glance took in the few remaining people. She added desperately, "I'll explain later—just get us out of here."

"I don't feel good," Dove mumbled. "I want to go home."

"Of course, honey," he said and put his arm around her shoulder, leading her up the aisle. Ann and Maddy followed close behind. Reverend Honeycutt was on their heels. Without a backward glance, the Sanders family left the church. But Ann knew it wasn't over; from the look of rapture she'd seen on the faces of most of the congregation, it was just the beginning.

"I'll be in touch," Reverend Honeycutt called after them, but no one seemed to hear him.

During the short drive home, Dove—pale and quiet—huddled in the backseat of the car next to Maddy. She felt strange—but that was probably because she'd fainted, she reasoned. How stupid! She'd never fainted in her life, and then she had to go and do it in front of all those people! She couldn't imagine what had come over her. Probably Mrs. Farley screaming in her ear. That was enough to make anyone faint!

Her father started to ask her a question, and Dove saw her mother touch his arm; he nodded. Just that little scene scared her even more. Why was her mother refusing to talk about it? Did that mean she thought Dove had something to do with that nutty business in the church? Well, she was having no part of it!

As soon as her father turned onto Lighthouse Lane, Dove spotted the familiar sandy-pink stucco house with its red-tiled roof. She jumped out of the car the minute it came to a stop and ran into the safety of her house and up the stairs to her room.

Ann followed Joe into the living room. "I'm going upstairs to talk to Dove. Maddy, let me talk to her first, and if she wants you, I'll let you know." Addressing Joe again, she said, "I'll be right down. I'll try to explain this fiasco."

"I'm not going anywhere," Joe answered, patting her arm.

While Dove changed into her nightgown, Ann studied her silently from the doorway. She heard Maddy's door close. Deciding to get straight to the point, Ann said, "Dove, I think we should discuss what happened at church tonight."

Dove shook her head, and Ann saw a flicker of fear in her daughter's eyes. "I'm tired, Mom, and I have a headache. I'd really like to go to sleep now. Let's talk tomorrow, okay?''

Ann sighed. "Would you like Maddy to sleep in your room tonight?''

On her hands and knees, looking under the bed for her kitten, Dove answered, "I'm okay, Mom, honest. I only fainted. No big deal. Paloma will keep me company.''

Ann hesitated a moment. "Do you want to talk to Maddy? I think she'd be better company than Paloma.''

Looking up at her from the floor, Dove repeated, "Really, Mom, I'm okay. Paloma will do fine.'' But Ann heard the quiver in Dove's voice.

Getting down on the floor beside her daughter, Ann took Dove in her arms. "It's all right to cry, honey. A good cry releases tension. And there was certainly plenty of that around tonight.''

Dove leaned into her mother and wept while Ann rocked her back and forth as if she were a small child. The anguish in Dove's sobbing tore at Ann's heart. She had never before seen her spirited daughter so emotionally drained. She realized that Dove's initial anger at being singled out had turned to fear. Perhaps it would be better to let the subject go until tomorrow, when Dove would feel stronger.

Finally, wiping her eyes with the back of her hand, Dove said: "I don't know what's the matter with me. Why am I crying like a baby?''

Stroking Dove's tangled hair, Ann soothed her daughter. "You're crying because you're angry, confused, frightened, and tired.'' So am I, Ann thought. "It's been a terribly emotional evening, honey. I'm not so sure anyone understands what happened tonight, least of all me. Talking about it will help sort things out, but a good night's sleep will probably do you more good. Everything will look different in the morning.'' Dear God, I hope so, she prayed silently.

Dove nodded, picked up Paloma, and climbed into bed.

" 'Night Mom," she whispered, tears clinging to her coppery lashes.

Ann ached to pull Dove back into her arms. A fierce possessiveness gripped her, making her want to lash out at anyone who would threaten her serene life. Yet she felt completely helpless, as useless as a broken toy. She didn't know how to reach out to Dove; she didn't know how to help her except to be there, to listen. Would that be enough?

Finally, Ann bent down and kissed her, murmuring, "I love you, honey," and then went to the door. Closing it softly, she walked down the hall to Maddy's room. Poor Maddy. She too was confused and scared and worried. And because everyone had been so concerned with Dove, Maddy had been forgotten.

After making sure Maddy was settled and assuring her that Dove was all right, Ann went downstairs. Joe was pacing the floor when she entered the living room. He stopped walking when he saw his wife and ran his hands through his reddish-brown hair.

"Okay, now tell me what happened. I couldn't make heads or tails out of Maddy's call. She sounded frantic. And just now, she wouldn't talk about it. Said she didn't know any more than what she told me on the phone and that you would explain. With that she practically flew up the stairs. So what's all this about a healing? And what has Dove got to do with it? And why did she faint?"

"I'm not sure I *know* what happened," Ann said wearily, sitting on the sofa. Joe settled beside her, taking her hands in his. "There *was* a healing—Genevieve Farley's arthritic hand. She got hysterical. Said Dove did it. . . ."

"Dove! Our little Miss Everything-About-Me-Is-Wrong?" Joe said with a grim laugh. When Ann didn't smile, he asked, "You don't believe it, do you?"

Ann hesitated. "I—I don't know, Joe. I really don't know. Dove denies it vehemently, and it does sound preposterous. But . . ."

Joe waited, but Ann said nothing. "But what?"

"Oh, Joe, it scares me," she said, sobbing into his shoulder. "There was the most—" She straightened and looked earnestly into his eyes. "She looked like an angel."

"Dove an angel!" Again his laugh faded. "How do you mean?"

"She *glowed*, Joe. She actually glowed." Ann stifled a sob. "Something profound happened. But I don't think Dove is aware of it—"

"How's Dove now?"

Ann shook her head. "I'm not sure. She doesn't want to talk. Not even to Maddy."

"Listen, Ann, the whole thing doesn't make any sense. Why would God choose someone like Dove? Wouldn't He pick someone more suited—more religious—or older—or something. . . ."

"Who knows the ways of God? His plan for Dove might go beyond what we are seeing now—maybe this is just a prelude to something He has in mind for her later. Oh, I don't know, Joe. I honestly don't know."

"Ann, I don't believe Dove had anything to do with the healing, but what if—by some strange fluke—she did have something to do with it? What will it mean?"

"I don't know. If it were Maddy I wouldn't be so concerned. She has a spirituality about her that would make it easy for her to handle a situation like this. But Dove . . ."

"That's the whole thing in a nutshell," Joe said. "She hates being different. If this thing turns out to be real—which I strongly doubt—well, you know she'll do everything in her power to try to undo things."

"But if she was responsible for Genevieve's healing, how will she undo that? Either she had something to do with it or she didn't, but either way it can't be changed."

"She'll find a way to prove she wasn't. Mark my words, Ann. She won't just sit back and get talked into this."

"But if God . . . ?"

Joe shook his head. "You're jumping to conclusions. Don't let the hysteria at church color your thinking."

Ann sighed. "Perhaps you're right. . . ."

"I am. You'll see."

While her parents were discussing the healing downstairs, up in her room Dove lay wide awake on the pink bedspread. Turning on her side, she pulled the kitten closer to her and ran her long fingers down its back. She stared at the soft white fur for a long time.

"I didn't even want to go to that dumb church," she told the kitten. "All I wanted to do was get my ears pierced." She looked at Paloma thoughtfully. "But you know what, Paloma? I do remember feeling some kind of tingling in my hand when I was holding Mrs. Farley's. First I got real hot, and then all the heat seemed to go into my hand." She shook her head. "Shoot. That old lady's probably a witch and put a spell on me." Dove spread her fingers wide and looked at them intently. "Look Paloma," she said, putting her hands in front of the kitten's face. "Just ordinary big hands—like any giant's."

Pushing the bedspread aside, Dove slipped under the sheets and snuggled the purring kitten to her. Before falling asleep she prayed that this whole horrid night was just a dream and that tomorrow everything would be back to normal. She sure hoped God was listening.

Dove woke up early, feeling uneasy. Something tugged at the back of her mind, but whenever it began to surface, she forced it down. Quickly pulling on green shorts and a sweatshirt over her bathing suit, she ran down the stairs two at a time, sneakers dangling from her hand. "Isn't Maddy up yet?" she asked her father, who was sipping coffee at the kitchen table.

Looking surprised, he put down his mug and glanced at his watch. "It's only seven. She's probably still asleep." He looked at Dove keenly. "Why are you up so early?"

"I want to take my new bike to the beach. And maybe ride around the island later on."

Joe nodded. "Okay, but don't go alone."

"I'll get Maddy to go with me," Dove called over her shoulder as she raced back up the stairs.

Just then the screen door slammed shut. Ann carried in an assortment of pink and yellow roses. "Was that Dove I heard?" she asked, reaching into the cabinet for a vase.

"It was. And she seems to be completely back to normal. Just as if nothing had happened last night." His voice carried an "I told you so" message.

"That's wishful thinking, Joe. Something did happen last night. Ignoring it isn't going to make it go away."

He rose from the chair and stood behind Ann, massaging her neck. "She'll be okay. She wants to take her new bike down to the beach. I told her not to go alone. If Maddy's with her, she'll be all right."

Ann nodded her head slowly. "I hope so." But inside she wasn't sure it was as simple as that.

Fifteen minutes later, Maddy and Dove barged into the kitchen. "Can I make some peanut butter and jelly sandwiches?" Dove asked her mother, laying her backpack on the floor. "We're going to have a picnic on the beach."

"What about breakfast?" Ann asked.

"We'll eat lunch early—like brunch."

Maddy poured pineapple juice into two glasses while Dove made the sandwiches.

"How are you feeling this morning, Dove?" Ann asked. She hoped her voice sounded casual, even as she covertly watched her daughter's face.

"Fine." But a sudden wariness crept into Dove's eyes. Obviously she had no intention of talking about last night. Well, give it a little more time. Perhaps the whole thing would blow over, as Joe said. For Dove's sake, she hoped so.

After putting a couple of bananas and oranges in a plastic bag and cold juice in a thermos, Dove zipped up the picnic sack. "Don't be too late." Ann said. "Dove, do you have a hat and suntan lotion? Maddy, make sure she doesn't fry to a crisp. You know your sister."

"Yes, Mom, yes," they chorused as they slipped out the screen door and headed for their new bicycles.

At the beach, they found a spot shaded by the giant branches of a palm tree a few feet from the low brick wall and sat down on the sand that was still cool and damp. Maddy opened the sandwiches, poured juice into paper cups, and handed one to Dove.

After a long silence, Maddy broached the subject. "Do you want to talk about last night?"

Dove shook her head vigorously while trying to swallow the peanut butter that had stuck to the roof of her mouth.

"I was scared, Dove. You were so white. I thought you were dying. . . ."

Finally Dove swallowed. "You kook. Why would I die? Just because some crazy old lady thinks I healed her. . . . I'm going swimming now." She dropped her sandwich, hastily removed her shorts and sweatshirt and ran into the water, leaving Maddy with the half-eaten food.

Dove didn't want to think about last night and all those people staring at her, let alone talk about it. If she could just keep her mind busy, she wouldn't have to think at all. Concentrating on her strokes, she swam for as long and as fast as she could. Then, exhausted, she dragged herself out of the water and fell on the blanket next to Maddy, who was absorbed in her book. Blocking out everything, Dove fell asleep.

A little while later, Maddy shook her sister's shoulder. "Hey, lazybones, you gonna sleep all day? I'd like some ice cream. Want to ride to the Sweet Tooth?"

Dove mumbled, "Only if I can have two scoops of chocolate chip."

"Fair enough," Maddy said, gathering the thermos and cups while Dove folded the blanket.

After locking their ten-speeds in front of the Sweet Tooth, the girls went into the ice cream parlor and sat at the counter. When they'd finished licking the last bit of chocolate from their spoons, they headed outside.

"It's one of them," Dove heard someone whisper. She turned around and saw three long-haired blond teenage boys straddling bicycles, staring at her and Maddy from the curb. An unexplained fear surged through Dove and she tried to free her bike, but she was unable to get the key in the lock. She began to panic without knowing why, and used the back of her hand to wipe the thin film of perspiration that had formed on her upper lip.

"Hey, which one of you is the healer?" a boy called out. The sound of the Beatles flowed from his transistor radio.

"Go take a long walk on a short pier, creep," Dove spat at the boy as she frantically tried to work the key. "Maddy, help me with this lock. We've got to get out of here."

Maddy looked at Dove's trembling hands and opened the lock for her. The girls mounted their bikes and began pedaling toward home.

"I bet it's the little dark one. That tall skinny one couldn't even open the lock," a voice taunted as the girls rode away.

"Har dee har har," Dove called bravely over her shoulder, even though she was unable to keep her voice from shaking.

"Let's follow them. I know where they live," another boy called out.

Panic and fear raced through Dove as she and Maddy pedaled home. When they reached the house, she dropped her bike on the front lawn and ran in, calling for her mother. Maddy followed her into the kitchen.

"What happened?" Ann asked as Dove threw herself into her mother's arms, sobbing.

"Some boys," Maddy gasped, out of breath.

"Did they do something to you?" Ann asked, looking from Dove to Maddy.

Maddy shook her head. "They wanted to know which one of us was the healer."

A knot of fear tightened in Ann as she tried to smooth

down Dove's flyaway hair. "Oh, honey, it's okay. Sit down. We're going to talk about this."

Feeling safe in her mother's presence, Dove sat down and dried her eyes with a paper napkin.

Suddenly they heard chanting outside. Dove turned a pasty white.

"We want to see the healer. We want to see the healer. We have a dead mouse we want her to heal."

Dove covered her ears with her hands. "Make them stop, Mom. Make them go away and leave me alone."

"Maddy, stay with your sister." Ann marched to the front door and stepped outside. "You leave my girls alone, do you hear?" she said firmly, glaring at the boys. "And get off my property or I'll call the police."

The boys turned their bikes around. "Go ahead, do it," one of the boys taunted his friend.

"Naw, you do it."

"Chicken!"

"Don't call me a chicken," he said as he threw a rubber mouse that landed on the porch.

Ann kicked it off. "Don't you ever come back here. If you do I'll have you arrested."

Earlier that morning, Genevieve Farley and Charlie Hale, the man who had been at church the night before, came by to see Dove. Ann had been relieved that Dove wasn't home. Now with those boys showing up on their doorstep, Ann didn't know how much longer she could protect Dove from the curious and the believers. Her whole body trembling, she walked back into the house, slamming the door behind her. Was today just the beginning?

She leaned over and kissed Dove's forehead. "They're gone now. They won't be back," she said. Dove bit her lip and nodded.

"As painful as it's going to be for you, Dove, we have to talk about what's happening. The island is too small for you to run away and hide every time someone mentions the healing. You're going to have to face it."

"But, Mom . . ."

"We're a family, Dove. And we're behind you one hundred percent. Maybe this will die down and go away. But you can't keep your feelings locked up inside you. That will only make the situation worse."

"I don't *know* what my feelings are, so how can I talk about them? Sometimes I hate Mrs. Farley, and then I feel bad because she couldn't help getting hysterical when she got healed. And I get mad at Reverend Honeycutt because he looked at me as if I was some kind of saint or something." Dove lowered her eyes. "I even hate you sometimes because you made me go. . . ."

"I understand how you feel, Dove. Look at me," Ann said, lifting Dove's chin. "Don't you know that I hate myself for making you go? That I'd give anything to be able to change last night's events? But that's not possible. So we have two choices—we either meet it head-on or we hide. Now where's my spunky little redhead?

"I don't know, Mom. The whole thing's so scary. Nothing like this has ever happened to me before. It was easy to be spunky when things were nice and normal. . . ."

"Changes are normal and part of growing up. Not all of them are nice. Many are painful. . . ."

"Dove," Maddy chimed in, "You've got to face what's happening. Stand up to them and show them your true colors. Don't turn away. That'll only make them want to taunt you more."

"Maddy's right," Ann said. "When someone is weak, people take advantage of that weakness. It's unfair, but that's how it is. Bluff your way through, if you have to. They won't know the difference."

Dove nodded thoughtfully.

Later, during dinner, Dove was thankful that her mother didn't bring up the subject of the healing, but her Dad kept watching her. Silence was beginning to acquire a new meaning for Dove—safety.

Suddenly there was a slam against the front door and

Dove jumped. Joe put his hand over his daughter's. "It's only the newspaper."

Relieved, she offered to get it and ran through the living room and out the door. When she stooped down to stare at the headline, she thought she was going to faint again. Each big black letter seemed to reach inside her and tear at her intestines.

"Dove?" Ann said behind her. She looked over her daughter's shoulder at the paper and gasped when she read the words: "CATALINA TEENAGER ALLEGEDLY DEMONSTRATES GIFT OF HEALING. It has been reported that last night during a local church service . . ."

Dropping the newspaper, Dove jumped to her feet and scurried past her mother, not thinking or feeling until she reached her room. She threw herself face down on the bed, pounding the pillow with her fists. "I'll get back at all those people who are doing this to me," she vowed. "Somehow I'll get even." But as she said the words, she knew she wouldn't do anything. She was quick to anger, but she was just as quick to forgive.

She rolled over and sat up, listening to Paloma's soft meowing from the corner of the room. She knelt down and scooped the kitten into her hands.

"I'm a real freak now, Paloma," she repeated over and over as she sat on the floor, rocking back and forth. "A real freak." Unable to hold back the tears any longer, she let them stream down her face.

Downstairs, Ann carried the newspaper into the dining room and speechlessly handed it to Joe.

Maddy paled as she read the headline over her father's shoulder. "Why are they doing this to her?" she asked, but her stunned parents didn't answer; they only shook their heads. "Why don't they leave her alone?" Maddy turned to her mother. "Dove hates attention, Mom. You know how she tries to go unnoticed. Now everyone on the island is going to be gawking at her. You have to stop them," she pleaded.

"I wish I knew how," Ann answered her daughter and looked to her husband for guidance. But Joe simply stared at the headline.

"I'm going up to talk to her," he said, pushing the chair away from the table and leaving Ann and Maddy staring at the uneaten food.

After tapping on Dove's door, Joe poked his head into her room. "You okay, honey?"

Looking out the balcony with her back to the door, Dove nodded, wishing he would go away.

"Just wanted to make sure you were all right. We're going to call Reverend Honeycutt and try to get this thing straightened out once and for all."

Turning, Dove walked over to her father. He took her hand in his. "I know how difficult this is for you, Dove, but we want you to know we love you and we're all behind you. You're not in this alone."

"Yes I am," she shouted angrily. "I'm the one who's different. I'm the one everyone's going to point at—and stare at. It's me who's the big, gawky freak!"

He opened his arms and Dove threw herself into his embrace. "I hate all this, Dad, but I don't know how to make it go away." Her teary face crumpled. "What are the kids at school going to think? For sure I'll never get a boy to look at me now."

"It'll probably blow over and be forgotten by then," Joe said, patting Dove's back.

"Do you really think so?"

Joe nodded. "Yup, I really do."

For a moment Dove experienced a ray of hope. But it didn't last long.

Suddenly she wanted to be alone. "I'm okay now, Dad. Thanks for coming up."

"Sure, honey." He opened his mouth to add something, but changed his mind and instead kissed the top of her russet hair before closing the door.

*   *   *

Dove sat on the floor with Paloma until it was dark. Without turning on the light, she undressed and got into bed. A shaft of moonlight illuminated her room, and she stared at the tiny silver stars painted on the pink ceiling. Even with her family's promises to stand behind her, Dove felt terribly alone.

An inner voice urged her to pray, but she knew it would be useless. God wasn't listening, at least not to her.

Chapter Four

It wasn't quite seven-thirty the next morning when the doorbell began its incessant ringing.

"I'm coming, I'm coming," Ann called from the kitchen. Placing her cup in the sink, she pushed back the black curls that had fallen on her forehead. "Now who in the world can this be so early?" she said aloud as she walked through the living room to the front door. "Better not be those boys and their pranks."

"Mrs. Sanders?" a young man asked.

"Yes. What can I do for you?"

"I'm Tim Franks—a reporter on the *Island News*." He pulled his identification card from his wallet and held it up. "If your daughter's home, I'd like to interview her."

Ann stared at him blankly.

"You know," he said, "the healing."

She stiffened. "There will be no interviews. That third-hand story in your newspaper last night was more than enough. I'm not going to allow my daughter to be subjected to this publicity. Now I'd appreciate it if you'd leave." She turned and started back into the house.

"But, Mrs. Sanders, this is an important story. Nothing like this has ever happened on the island as far as I know. Your daughter could become famous. . . ."

Ann faced him again. "She doesn't want to be famous.

41

She just wants to be left alone." Her protective stance added finality to her words.

"If you change your mind, will you call me?"

Ann didn't answer.

"Here's my number anyway," he said and thrust a card into her hand.

Ann walked into the house without a backward glance.

Sitting down wearily at the kitchen table, she crushed the card with trembling fingers. She had hoped things would quiet down, but instead they were going haywire. The last thing Dove needed was to be interviewed. What she really needed was to be left alone. But that didn't seem to be possible.

Last night when she'd called Reverend Honeycutt, she'd gotten the same feeling: No one seemed to have any control over the situation. It was snowballing and getting completely out of hand. The minister was so excited about having a *miracle* during his healing service that he was having a hard time concentrating on Dove and her problems. It seemed as if he too had gotten caught up in the hysteria. Ann hoped it was temporary.

Yesterday it was the teenagers. Today it was a newspaper reporter. What would tomorrow bring? Television cameras? She was staring into space when Maddy walked into the room.

"I heard the doorbell. Who was it?" Stopping abruptly, Maddy looked at Ann's stunned face and asked, "Mom, are you all right?" She put her arms around her mother. "What's wrong? You look like you've seen a ghost!"

"I'm okay." Ann smiled wanly. "Some reporter wanted to interview Dove. I told him to leave."

Maddy nodded agreement.

"We have to protect Dove," Ann continued.

"Dove's stronger than we give her credit for, Mom. She's a survivor."

"Do you really think so? You're closer to her than anyone else. At least you were before this happened. . . ."

Maddy smiled. "You'll see."

"Where is she now?"

"In her room, probably wondering how she ever got into such a pickle."

It was Ann's turn to smile. "Keep an eye on her, will you, Maddy? She's so sensitive to others' opinions." Ann pitched the crumpled card into the garbage.

"I will. Don't worry, Mom." Maddy took the milk carton from the refrigerator and poured some into a large glass. "I think I'll take some up to Dove," she said and scooped a whopping tablespoon of Ovaltine into a second glass. "Maybe she's ready to talk."

Ann sighed as she watched Maddy carry the milk upstairs.

"Dove, my hands are full. Open the door for me," Maddy called.

A tousle-haired Dove groped her way to the door and opened it. Stretching, she asked, "What time is it?"

"Almost eight. You sleep too much."

Dove reached for the darkened milk and sat on the edge of her bed. "Sometimes sleeping is better than being awake." She sipped the milk. "Who was at the door so early this morning? The dumb bell woke me up."

"Mom said it was a reporter."

Dove tightened her grip on the glass so it wouldn't slip through her fingers. "Reporter? Why?"

"He said he wanted to interview you." Maddy sat down on the bed next to Dove.

"Why would anybody want to interview me?"

Maddy pushed the pillow aside. "You know why. Don't play Miss Innocent."

"I don't know what you're talking about." She locked her gaze on the foamy milk.

"Yes you do, Dove. One, Mrs. Farley's hand was healed. Two, you were holding it. Three, now everyone thinks you had something to do with the healing."

Dove shook her head in denial. "But I didn't, Maddy." She put her glass on the night table next to the bed and crossed her legs tailor fashion. "Anyone could have been holding her hand when it happened. Just because it was me doesn't mean I had anything to do with the healing. I'm not even religious—you know that.''

"Some people are spiritual without being religious.''

"Now what the heck does that mean?'' Dove demanded.

"It means they have a closeness to God, without being obvious.''

"You mean like talking to God as if He was a friend?'' she asked, and Maddy nodded. Dove was thoughtful. "Well, I'm not talking to God anymore.''

"Why not?''

Dove squirmed but defiantly met Maddy's shocked eyes. "Because I asked Him to make this big mess go away and He didn't.''

"Dove, don't you know yet that God always knows what's best for us?''

"He doesn't this time,'' Dove said emphatically.

"Dove!'' Maddy straightened her back, horrified at her sister's words.

"You see, I'm not very spiritual either, am I?'' Tears of frustration began to roll down her face. Why couldn't she do anything right lately? She was downright miserable, and everyone else seemed to be just as bad off—and all because of her. Is this what happens when you turn fifteen?

Maddy grabbed a tissue and wiped Dove's tears away. "Maybe God's testing you.''

"Well, if He is, this is one test I'm definitely going to fail. And without even trying,'' she said as she held back more tears.

Maddy sighed in exasperation. "Why don't you just go along with it? You know, stop fighting God and everyone else and see what happens.''

"Never,'' Dove said in a whisper. "I had nothing to do with Mrs. Farley's healing, and no one will ever make me think different.'' She toyed with the jar of Clearasil lying on the night table.

"Dove, we're not communicating at all. I'm talking and you're denying.''

"And what am I supposed to do? Go along with everything you say?" Her eyes blazed as she glared at her sister. "We're not talking about hairstyles and new clothes, you know. And we're not talking about you, the pretty Madonna look-alike who's perfect. We're talking about me," she lashed out, pointing to herself. "Me! The freak! The ugly duckling!"

"Oh, Dove, you're none of those terrible things," Maddy said, putting an arm around her sister. "I'm sorry if I sounded like I was nagging you. I was only trying to help." Suddenly Maddy's eyes filled with tears.

"Now don't you start crying," Dove said, wishing she could take back the horrible words she'd said to Maddy.

"I'm not crying, silly. I just feel—emotional," she said lamely. "Meanwhile, back at the ranch . . ."

Dove looked skeptical. "Okay. What's coming next?"

"Mom and Dad are worried about you. The way you've been acting since the service."

"I'm sorry for that. I really am. Maybe there was a miracle, Maddy, but it had nothing to do with me. Why is that so hard for people to understand? Especially my own mother. Dad seems to be on my side sometimes, but then he gets swayed by Mom." Dove got up and walked to the balcony door; the bay outside seemed to be beckoning to her.

Maddy didn't give up. "But how can you be so sure you had nothing to do with it?"

Dove raised her eyebrows and shrugged. She had had enough of this topic. Suddenly she couldn't take any more. She had to get out of the house.

"I think I'll go for a bike ride. Tell Mom, okay?"

Maddy nodded and walked over to Dove. "Want me to go along?"

"I think I'd rather go alone this time. Do you mind?"

"No, of course not. I just thought maybe you'd like some company." She picked up the empty glasses and left.

Dove's gaze followed her sister's retreating back. Now it seemed she couldn't say or do anything without feeling guilty. Was this also part of growing up? Ugh, she thought. I'd rather do without it.

She dressed quickly and took the stairs two at a time. She avoided the kitchen so she wouldn't have to hear about the reporter.

Looking up at the sky, Dove saw that traces of clouds filtered the sun. Good thing; she'd forgotten her suntan lotion. She pedaled to Descanso Bay, knowing the small beach would be deserted at such an early hour. Chaining her bike, she walked to a spot by a large palm tree.

She sat with her back against the wide palm, its shadow protecting her from the intermittent morning sun. Several sailboats were anchored in the distance, and their bobbing motion, together with the sound of the waves pushing and pulling, had a hypnotizing effect on Dove.

She closed her eyes. Suddenly her thoughts raced back to the Little Church on the Hill and the healing service. She tried to push them back into the recesses of her mind, but she had vivid recall of the fateful evening.

The memory of the heat in her hand, the hysterical words spoken and the curious stares directed toward her at the service all came rushing back and began to suffocate her.

Frightened by the scenes her mind replayed, she knew she had to focus on something else. Something pleasant, exciting. Searching her mind, she thought about the beautiful fish she'd seen when snorkeling a few weeks ago. She let her mind wander until she felt calm.

A few minutes later she opened her eyes and saw two teenage boys walking toward her. She picked up a small stick, bowed her head and began writing in the sand, hoping they wouldn't notice her. Under lowered lashes, she watched their approach. One of the boys was eleventh-grader Bob Anderson. She didn't know the other one. After yesterday's episode with the long-haired creeps on bikes, Dove cringed at the thought of a similar encounter.

"Hey, red," the dark-haired boy she didn't recognize called out as he neared. "Where's that cute sister of yours?'' Dove made believe she didn't hear him, but the hurt was deep. Wasn't there anything nice about *her* for a boy to notice? Yet at the same time relief flooded her. Questions about Maddy she could handle. When they were closer, he said, ''Aren't you the one everyone's talking about? Something about a healing. . . .''

Her moment of relief vanished in an explosion of fear. ''Oh, God, make them go away,'' she murmured under her breath, lowering her head in embarrassment. Maybe if she ignored them, they'd walk by without stopping. It was worth a try.

''Did you really bring a dead mouse back to life?'' the dark-haired boy asked in mock seriousness. Dove's face burned hotly and her stomach churned. She wanted desperately to sink into the sand.

''Cool it, Johnson. Leave her alone,'' Bob Anderson said, apparently aware of Dove's discomfort. Grabbing the other boy's arm, Bob propelled him away from her.

When she was sure they were gone, Dove leaned back, resting her head against the tree, and thanked Bob Anderson silently for getting the jerk away from her. She tried not to think, but she didn't seem to have any control over the questions that suddenly loomed in her mind. Whatever possessed Mrs. Farley to sit next to her when there were several empty pews in the church? Was it possible God had ordained it? She shook her head in denial. No, she couldn't accept that. Because the minute she did, her life would change. And she didn't want it to—at least not in that way.

If God wanted to change her, why didn't He do something with the color of her hair or maybe shorten her feet a size or two? Dove smiled at her wishful thinking, but her face sobered when she looked down at her hands and remembered the tingling sensation. Could they possibly have been instrumental in a healing? She moved her fingers. Perfectly normal. Her hand wasn't hot now. It was just the same oversized hand it had always been. Certainly if she had any special powers she'd see it—feel it—know it. Yet all it was was the same familiar hand. Not bigger, not smaller, just the same old giant hand.

She remembered when Maddy fell last week and skinned her knee. She had touched Maddy's knee, wiped the blood off with a tissue, and put on a Band-Aid, and nothing unusual had happened. If this was a magic healing hand, then Maddy's skinned knee would have gotten better right away. Instead it had hurt for days.

I have to walk, Dove thought. I must keep moving. Anything to stop these stupid thoughts. She stood and walked the length of the small beach several times, hearing the sand squeak under her sneakers and feeling the hot sun on her skin. "I'll probably burn," she thought and then giggled when another thought came to her. "Oh, well, I'll just heal away the sunburn." Realizing it was not a laughing matter, she forced all such unbidden ideas from her mind. Whenever one tried to intrude, she'd pick up a pebble and throw it as far and as wide as she could into the water. Physical movement helped ease the tension building up in her. She wished she'd remembered to bring her snorkeling equipment.

Finally, she pedaled home, thoughts of church and healing shoved into the background by hunger pangs for lunch. Slipping into the kitchen unnoticed, Dove poured a glass of milk and started making a sandwich. As she ran her finger over the knife to capture a dollop of peanut butter, she was suddenly aware of murmurings coming from the living room. The low male voice was familiar, yet for the moment she couldn't identify it. She stood motionless, trying to match the face with the voice.

Her heart began to pound when she recognized Reverend Honeycutt's voice, now slightly raised. She didn't want to hear what he was saying, yet she was powerless to move.

"Ann," the minister said, "I must talk to Dove. If she has been given the gift of healing, it must be used to help others."

Dove covered her ears with her hands in an attempt to

block out the words she refused to accept. But her mother's voice filtered through and she let her hands fall to her sides.

"Look. We go to church on Sundays and we have a family Bible. And sometimes I volunteer at church functions. But so does just about everyone else in the congregation." Ann paused, then continued, "This whole thing doesn't make any sense. Why would Dove, who knows absolutely nothing about healing, be given such a gift? Why?"

"It's not always for us to know the answers. Some things must be taken in faith. The truth is, Ann, your daughter held Genevieve Farley's hand during the Lord's Prayer and . . ."

"I know. I know. We've been over that a million times already, Reverend. But maybe she would have been healed anyway, with or without Dove holding her hand. Have you ever thought of that?" Dove could hear a touch of pleading in her mother's voice.

"That's a distinct possibility," Reverend Honeycutt admitted. "And that's why I want to talk to Dove. She needs to know if she's been blessed with the gift of healing. For that reason, I'd like to try to persuade her to come to our next healing service."

"And have everyone gaping at her? Do you know, Reverend, she already feels uncomfortable because she's taller than the other kids her age and because of her red hair. What you suggest certainly won't make her feel like she fits in with her peers. What it will do is alienate her even more—even if it's only in her own mind. I can't allow it," she finished firmly.

"You'd go against the wishes of God?"

Dove put her hand to her mouth to stifle the cry that rose in her throat. I detest you, she thought fiercely. It's not fair saying that kind of stuff to scare us.

"I'm sorry, Reverend, but I can't see any proof that God is behind this," Ann said flatly. "I'm not convinced that He has given Dove the gift of healing. This whole thing could be just a coincidence. Now you have to admit that, Reverend Honeycutt.''

"Well, yes, it could be. But how are we to know one way or the other if we don't talk to Dove?'' He sighed and hesitated. Then in a low voice he continued, "And was it a coincidence that you named your daughter *Dove*, which is the symbol of the Holy Spirit?''

Ann shook her head in exasperation. "Oh, come now, Reverend. It was just a pretty name. I've always disliked having such a common name myself and wanted my daughters called something different—something exotic. My choosing the name Dove had nothing to do with the Holy Spirit.''

"How can you be so sure, Ann? Maybe God had something to do with the names you chose.''

Hearing the minister's ridiculous suggestions, Dove wished with all her might that God would come down and straighten out this mess. Softly she walked toward the entranceway that led to the dining room, but stopped and stood behind the arch where she could see into the living room without being seen.

Ann rose and nervously faced the minister. "Let's get back to facts. What can Dove tell you that you don't already know? I've told you everything that happened. She won't talk about it. Not to me—not to her father—not even to her twin sister. And if she does talk to you, what can she possibly say that will make any difference?''

"If she's been given the gift, we'll know.''

"How?'' Ann demanded.

Reverend Honeycutt shrugged his broad shoulders. "There will be an aura about her, a presence.''

Ann's laugh was bitter. "My daughter certainly hasn't sprouted wings since all this happened. Actually, she's become withdrawn and silent. She definitely hasn't become saintly. I doubt if I'll be able to get her to set foot inside a church again. You won't learn anything from talking to her.''

"Why don't you let me try, Ann? Maybe I can get her to loosen up and talk about it."

"What makes you think you'll have more success with my daughter than I've had?" Tired and frustrated, Ann said, "And just how many *miracles* have you witnessed, Reverend Honeycutt?" Dove knew by the stricken expression on her mother's face that she regretted the words as soon as they were spoken.

He cleared his throat. "Well, actually, I haven't witnessed any physical healings before Genevieve's, but I've been a minister for many years and I know a lot about healing."

"This is getting us nowhere," Ann said wearily. Shaking her head, she sat down again.

Dove heard the fatigue in her mother's voice and saw the pain in her eyes. She realized that she wasn't the only one who was suffering—her entire family was. Part of her wanted to run out the back door to escape, but a stronger part urged her toward the living room. Dove found herself taking one step after another until she was standing in the doorway. Her mother looked up.

"Dove!"

"It's okay, Mom. I heard everything. I'll talk to Reverend Honeycutt." She looked over at him. "Then he'll see it was all a dumb mistake."

"Come sit by me," Ann said, patting the cushion beside her. Dove sank down wearily, dreading what she couldn't understand.

A large fan cooled the Sanders living room. Reverend Honeycutt sat across from Dove. He reached for her hands, but Dove pulled back.

"Dove," he said kindly, "do you have any idea how many people you could help if you do have the gift of healing?"

Dove stared defiantly at him. "I don't have any gift— and I don't want any, either."

"Okay," he said quickly, trying not to antagonize her.

"Why don't you tell me about your relationship with God then."

Dove thought for a moment. "I'm not sure I have one. I'm not religious, you know. Not like Maddy. I used to talk to God like a friend—but not anymore."

"Why is that?"

"Because of what He did to me. He made me the town freak." Her eyes filled with tears.

"Not a freak—but a very special young lady."

Dove shook her head and hot tears slid down her cheeks. Ann tried to put her arm around Dove, but she pulled away.

It was obvious this strategy wasn't going the way Reverend Honeycutt had expected. Ann watched him struggle to find the right words.

When Dove wiped her eyes, the minister continued in a soft voice, "Dove, I want you to think back to Tuesday night and tell me everything you thought—everything you remember. Don't leave anything out even if you feel it might sound silly. It's important we know all the details so we can get to the bottom of this matter."

Ann gave her daughter a quick glance, and Dove nodded to the minister. With a deep sigh, she began slowly.

"Well, actually I didn't want to go to church." It was important to Dove that he know that. "It was our birthday—Maddy's and mine—and we wanted to go to the movies or do something for fun. But Mom wanted to go to the service. She conned us into going by taking us to get our ears pierced first." Dove involuntarily touched an earring, then shrugged. "So we went along with it."

Dove looked from her mother to the minister. "But I knew something was going to happen. I felt . . . weird."

"In what way?" Reverend Honeycutt asked.

"Oh, sort of like I was anxious or something. My hands were all sweaty before I even got into church."

"That's because you were nervous, Dove," Ann said. "Remember? You asked me if it was going to be scary."

"I remember, but still I had a funny feeling. You know, strange—different."

Reverend Honeycutt leaned forward expectantly.

"I didn't even listen to your sermon. I remember looking at the stained glass windows, wondering if maybe Maddy would make one some day. I remember wishing I was at the movies, and I wondered if my ear was bleeding—you know, things like that. Then you said we were all to stand and hold hands. I remember how I . . ." She almost said how she found it repulsive to hold that withered, gnarled hand. ". . . how we all started to sing. That's when my hand felt hot—and I got lightheaded—like I might faint. When the hymn was over, my hand didn't feel hot anymore—just normal. Like now." She shook her hand to show him and let it drop slowly onto her lap. Suddenly her voice changed and became softly lyrical. "I remember feeling calm—real quiet-like—sort of light and airy. The church seemed—oh, I don't know how to explain it—peaceful, I guess. . . ."

Ann stared in stunned disbelief as an ethereal glow seemed to suffuse Dove's features. She was unable to look anywhere but at her daughter's gentle face.

It was apparent that Dove was oblivious to her surroundings; she spoke as if she were in a trance. Ann's eyes were drawn to her daughter's long, slender fingers that lay quietly on her lap. For some reason, Ann felt like crying.

When Dove stopped speaking, Reverend Honeycutt cleared his throat as if to regain control of his emotions. "Dove," he asked softly, leaning closer to her, "what do you think happened in church that night?"

Dove looked around and pushed her hair behind her ears before speaking. Why was Reverend Honeycutt asking that question when she'd just told him everything?

Ann saw the familiar gesture as a sign that Dove had recovered from whatever it was that had taken her so far away.

"Well, anybody could see that Mrs. Farley's hand was healed," Dove said crossly. "But I had nothing to do with it. My holding her hand was just a coincidence. If God was going to heal her, He didn't need my help. It would've happened no matter who held her hand. You're all just getting excited over nothing. I told you before—I'm not a healer. I'm just . . ." She almost said, *a redheaded freak*. Instead she ended, ". . . I'm just—me."

Reverend Honeycutt seemed to notice the change and reversed his tactics. Placing his large hands on his knees, he leaned forward. "Okay, Dove, perhaps it was a coincidence. We have no way of knowing that now, do we? I mean, we have no proof, right?"

Dove nodded.

"A miracle happened. We don't question that. What we haven't proved is whether you were instrumental in the healing." He sighed deeply. "You know, Dove, it seems to me there's only one way to find out if you have the gift of healing or not." Dove watched him expectantly, weighing his words. "If it was a coincidence, as you seem to think, then what do you have to lose by coming to our service next week? You won't have to do anything different from what you did last Tuesday. What do you say?"

Ann held her breath. After seeing the change in Dove's face when she spoke of the healing service, she didn't know what to think.

Dove looked at her mother for direction.

"It's up to you, dear," Ann said gently.

"Will you and Dad and Maddy be there with me?"

"Of course we will." Ann wanted desperately to take her daughter in her arms and hold her, protect her. She looked at Reverend Honeycutt. "If Dove decides to do this, I don't want anyone else to know she's going to be at that service. Otherwise it might turn into a circus."

"I agree."

It was the only way to prove she had nothing to do with Mrs. Farley's healing, Dove thought, and to end all this crazy talk. She stood up and said, "Okay. I'll do it."

Chapter Five

Relief flooded through Dove as soon as she made her decision. After next Tuesday's church service, her life would return to normal. She vowed never again to complain about anything if God would only clear up this horrible mess.

She turned to her mother and asked, "Where's Maddy?"

"Probably out in the shed working on her stained glass."

"Excuse me, please," Dove said politely, and Reverend Honeycutt nodded.

Ann watched her go and then addressed the minister. "I know Dove said she'd attend next week's service, but if she changes her mind in the meantime I won't force her. It has to be her decision at all times."

He nodded. "I agree. But after what I saw today, I don't expect she'll change her mind." He rose and went over to Ann and sat down beside her. He took her hand in his and said softly, "I strongly suspect there is more going on here than we can understand."

Ann nodded. Yes, she had seen the change come over Dove too. Yet why did she feel numb, as if expecting something terrible to happen? She knew that if the gift had been given to Maddy she'd feel differently. Maddy was the logical one to receive such an honor. She was docile, sensitive, and open—she accepted everything without complaint. And suddenly Ann realized that Maddy was very close to God, while Dove seemed to be worlds away from Him.

Confused, she wondered if there was a logic behind God's working in their lives that they didn't always recognize. She didn't know.

She only knew that until this week, her life had been extremely simple. From the day she'd married Joe Sanders, everything had seemed to fall neatly into place. During his last semester at UCLA, he had sent résumés to the Catalina hotels and was offered a job as assistant manager of El Sol, a small hotel in Avalon. They moved to the island right after graduation, and Ann found work as a receptionist at the St. Catherine Hotel. When the twins were born, she retired from the working world. Joe moved up quickly and was soon able to turn his job into a partnership at El Sol, and their life continued smoothly, without friction. Until now.

The pressure of the minister's hand on hers brought Ann back to her living room and the kindly face watching her. She nodded again, slowly, Then they both rose, and she walked the burly minister to the front door.

"I'll see you at seven next Tuesday," he said as he walked down the porch steps.

"You won't mention to anyone that Dove plans to attend the service, will you?" Ann reminded him.

"You have my word."

Ann stood watching the car move away, then turned and walked back into the house, closing the door softly behind her.

Throwing open the door of the shed, Dove suddenly stopped. "Oh, I didn't mean to come barging in. I mean, I didn't know Allen was here. . . ."

"No problem. I was just showing him the sunset I finished making this morning. What do you think?" Maddy held the stained glass up to the light.

Dove didn't miss the fact that Allen was paying more

attention to Maddy than to her work of art. She sighed, wondering if anyone would ever look at her like that. She hoped so, but doubted it.

"Not bad for an amateur," Dove said with a twinge of jealousy in her voice. It wasn't fair that Maddy had both the looks and the talent. *And* the boyfriend.

Allen walked over to Maddy and put his hands on her shoulders. "Have to go to track practice now. Gotta keep in shape for my last year in school. See you tomorrow." He pushed a blond strand of hair off his forehead.

Maddy smiled and told him good-bye. Dove raised her hand in a half-hearted salute.

Maddy turned to her sister. "Did you want to talk?"

"You always know everything, don't you?" Dove retorted, instantly regretting her sarcasm.

"Not everything," Maddy wrapped the newly made sunset in tissue and put it on a shelf.

"Well, I do want to talk to you. Guess who's at the house?"

Maddy shrugged. "Another reporter?"

"No. Reverend Honeycutt."

"What's he doing at our house?"

"He wanted to talk to me."

"And did he?"

Dove nodded. After explaining to Maddy what had happened, she said, "So I decided to go." She picked up a piece of red glass and held it up to the light.

"Well, I guess we'll know one way or the other on Tuesday, won't we?"

Dove all but slammed the piece of glass on the table. "It's not a matter of knowing *one way or the other,* Maddy. Tuesday night everyone will know I had *nothing to do* with Mrs. Farley's stupid healing."

"Dove, healings aren't stupid. Do you always have to use such words as dumb and stupid and weird? Especially where God is concerned?"

Turning her palms upward and shrugging, Dove said, "Okay, okay. So healing isn't stupid, but Mrs. Farley is definitely weird. And that preacher is dumb, thinking I'm a healer. I'm the last one God would pick on. I'll sure be glad when this is over and things get back to the way they were." She laughed. "And I used to complain then. No more. I've learned my lesson. Be happy with what you have because it's better than what you might get."

Maddy cringed. "Oh, Dove, where did you ever get such a philosphy?"

Dove looked at her sister quizzically. "Philosophy? I didn't even know I had one."

"Well, you do. But let's hope it'll change as you get older." She shook her head sadly. "With that type of thinking, what kind of future can you look forward to? You're stopping all the wonderful things that could happen to you. . . ."

"The only wonderful things I ever wanted to happen to me," Dove interrupted, "were having ordinary brown hair, being four inches shorter, and wearing a size five shoe."

Maddy shook her head impatiently. "Oh, Dove, those aren't the kinds of things I'm talking about. I'm talking about meaningful things. Your life, your future—where you want to go—what you want to do—and more important, who you are as a person."

"You're too deep for me, Maddy. All I want in my future is to meet a cute guy, get married, have kids, and have a snorkeling shop on the side. What do I need to do to get that?"

"I guess nothing. If that's what you really want, it'll happen." Maddy closed her eyes for a moment as if to sort out what she was going to say next. "Dove," she said quietly, "I think we got off the subject."

"What do you mean?" Dove asked nervously, pushing a strand of hair behind her ears.

"I mean—what happens if you go to church Tuesday and someone gets healed again."

"That won't happen. It just won't." She crossed her fingers behind her back.

"Dove, you're not looking past your nose."

"Oh, come off it, Maddy. You sound just like Mom."

Maddy ignored her sister's comment. "I have this strong feeling. You know how sometimes I get intuitions? Well, I get the feeling that you've been given the gift of healing. And if you have, you must use it," Maddy said earnestly. "Healing might be your mission in life."

"Mission! Look, Maddy, I'm not into missions or any of that churchy stuff. I don't have a gift from God and *I don't want one.*"

Maddy put her hand on Dove's shoulder. "I'm just trying to be of help by telling you what I feel."

"I don't want to know what you feel. I don't want to hear about intuitions and philosophies and missions and all that mumbo jumbo." Her voice took on a note of hysteria as she clenched her fists and glared. "You like all that mystical stuff. I don't. It scares me, Maddy, and I hate it. It makes me shake all over, even inside." She hugged herself tightly.

"But if it's a gift from God . . . ." Maddy persisted, her hand sliding down Dove's arm.

"I . . . don't . . . want . . . it," Dove enunciated, shaking off Maddy's hand. "I just want to be left alone. Can't you understand that? I'm different than you are and I can't help how I am." Suddenly, she laughed a sad little laugh. "It's really all God's fault. He must have got our genes mixed up." She walked out of the shed when she felt tears rolling down her cheeks, and hastened to her room.

Dove hated having words with Maddy. They almost never argued, and Dove was smart enough to know that the reason had more to do with Maddy's disposition than with hers. There were times when she was convinced that a rotten temper went along with her awful red hair—and this was definitely one of those times.

And that's what was so strange about this whole thing. Maddy was sweet and gentle, the kind who should get a gift from God. Yet everyone kept insisting that *she* was the one.

Suddenly Dove's face brightened. Of course! she thought. In a flash she knew exactly what had happened. She'd had nothing to do with the healing. No, the healing had flowed from Maddy's hand through Dove's to Mrs. Farley's. Why hadn't she realized that earlier? It explained everything. But she decided not to let anyone else in on her secret just yet. She'd set up some kind of test for Tuesday.

Formulating a foolproof plan wasn't as easy as she'd thought. Unless Maddy stayed home, she'd be somewhere in the chain of hands. But perhaps if there were two or three people between her and Maddy it would weaken the power to heal. She'd try it. Without explaining why, she'd ask her mom and dad to sit next to her.

Feeling freer than she had in days, Dove flung open the balcony doors and gazed out. In the distance she could see the Bay of Avalon with lines of brightly colored sailboats bobbing up and down. Her mom loved Catalina for its red-tile-roofed houses, its hilly paths, and its flowering shrubs, but Dove loved Catalina for its calm waters and tiny beaches.

For the past couple of days, she'd been blind to the very things that made her home town so special, but now that she had cleared up the mystery, she was able again to appreciate the wonders that surrounded her on every side. Turning back toward her bedroom, she glanced at the clock on her night table. It was still early enough to ride to the beach and get in a little snorkeling.

Dove changed into a bathing suit and pulled on her shorts and a shirt. "I'm going to the beach for a while," she said brightly, stopping a second to give her mother a noisy kiss on the cheek as she ran through the kitchen.

"Have a good time," Ann called to Dove's retreating back. "Now that sounded like the Dove I used to know," she said aloud, smiling.

After collecting her snorkeling gear from the shed, Dove pedaled to Crescent Beach. Everything looks terrific now, she thought as she kicked off her sneakers and stepped onto the warm summer sand. Squirming out of her shorts, she ran into the water, its cool wetness enveloping her. A few minutes later, she ran back for her mask and snorkel.

It was wonderful looking through the clear blue water at the fish swimming around her. They didn't seem to be afraid, only curious. When she began to feel cold, Dove swam back to the beach and sat on the sand to catch her breath. When her breathing returned to normal, she stood up and dried herself off with her beach towel and then wrapped it around her like a sarong. Digging into the pockets of her shorts, she found enough money for an ice cream cone and walked to the pier. She licked the cone as she sauntered back to her spot on the beach.

"All by yourself?" a voice asked.

Startled, she turned to look up at Bob Anderson. Amazing, she thought; I actually have to look *up* at someone. Too shy to speak, she nodded.

"Want to sit?" he asked.

Dove couldn't believe this was happening. A real live boy—and a junior too—wanted to be with her. Now *this* was what she called a miracle! "Sure, why not," she answered.

They sat on the sand in front of the low wall that ran along the beach and stared straight ahead, neither of them speaking. The soft murmur of the waves lapping at their feet and the laughter of children playing ball in the water were the only sounds. Dove tried to run her fingers through her matted hair and wipe the sand off her legs, but it was useless. Her hair seemed to be glued together, and the sand stuck to her legs, refusing to budge.

"I heard what happened at church the other night."

End of miracle.

"I thought you might like to know," he continued, "that I think it's pretty cool to have something like that happen."

She looked at him. "That's because it didn't happen to you."

"What do you mean?" A slight frown furrowed his forehead. He wasn't making fun of her. He was serious.

"Well, I feel like everyone is always staring at me—waiting for me to do something—you know, miraculous. But I'm just an ordinary girl and I just do ordinary things." Shrugging, she turned her hands palms up.

"Not so ordinary." Then as if his words embarrassed him, he looked out over the bay.

Dove felt her heart thudding. Did he mean *she* wasn't ordinary, or her hands weren't ordinary? He said it as if it was a compliment, and she wanted to think he meant it that way. She glanced at him out of the corner of her eye. He was really good-looking. Tan, with sun-streaked blond hair that reached the collar of his shirt. She couldn't see his eyes, but she knew they had to be dark blue, like the ocean he was staring at. He was new in Avalon; his father worked at the bank. Of course, when new families moved into town, everyone soon knew all about them.

"Your name's Dove, isn't it?"

She nodded.

"That's a pretty unusual name. But then I guess you are, too."

"I am too what?" Pretty? she asked silently.

"Unusual."

She made a face.

"You just don't seem like the other girls at school. You seem more . . ." He hesitated and then blurted out: ". . . fiery."

Dove giggled. "That's because of my red hair." Suddenly she liked the color of her hair. She liked talking to Bob Anderson. He made her feel special, and she liked that very much.

"You a sophomore this year?" he asked.

"Uh huh. And you'll be a junior, right?"

"Right." He glanced at his watch and stood up. "I have to go now. I'm supposed to be on an errand for my mom. Which beach do you usually hang out on? This one or Descanso?"

"Both. And sometimes Pebbly Beach."

"Yeah, but if I want to see you again, which beach should I look for you on?"

Her heart started acting up again. He actually wanted to see her. Her. Dove Sanders. She was staring, but no words came out.

"If you have a boyfriend . . ." he stammered.

His words immediately brought her to her senses. "No, I don't have a boyfriend. Not right now, anyway," she qualified. "I come here mostly. Early in the morning before the tourists invade us."

Bob laughed, and the sound made Dove feel good inside. "Well, maybe I'll see you here." He picked up his sneakers and began walking away.

"Are you staying on the island the whole summer?" she called after him.

"Sure thing," he said and waved.

She watched him walk to the street and stared after his tall, slender frame until he was out of sight. Even when she couldn't see him anymore, she continued looking. Then with an enormous sigh, she lay back on the sand and repeated every word he'd said. Well, if he didn't see her it wouldn't be through any fault of hers. She planned to be on the beach *every single morning* at eight—just in case.

Too excited to stay still a second longer, she jumped up, brushed the sand off her suit, grabbed her things, and ran to her bike. She couldn't wait to tell Maddy and her mom. "Yahoo!" she hollered as she stuffed everything into the basket.

This must be what it's like to fly, Dove thought as she pedaled energetically to her house, her tangled hair blowing in the breeze and her spirits soaring. Leaning her bike against the porch, she raced up the stairs and into the kitchen. "Mom! Where are you? I need to talk to you. Maddy?" Finding no one in the kitchen, she took off for the living room. Empty. She stood with her hands on her hips and then pushed her hair behind her ears. "Wouldn't you know it. Just when I have exciting news, there's no one around to tell it to."

"Dove, is that you? We're up in Maddy's room," her mother called.

Stumbling in an effort to take the stairs three at a time, she nevertheless reached Maddy's bedroom in record time. Astonished faces stared at her from the closet door as she flopped on the bed, a huge grin spread across her face.

"What're you two doing?" she asked.

"Cleaning out Maddy's closet. Yours is next. Why the grin from ear to ear?" Ann asked, sitting down on the bed.

Dove bounced on the bed, unable to sit still. "I'm not saying until Maddy puts down those clothes and comes over here."

Maddy crossed to the bed and sat beside Dove. "Okay. Let's hear it."

"I'm in love!"

Ann burst into laughter as relief flooded through her. She hadn't known what to expect. "You've only been gone an hour and you're in love?"

"Oh, Dove. Who? How? Where?" Maddy asked grabbing her sister's leg and squeezing it.

Dove sat up. She gazed dreamily from her mother to her sister and sighed rapturously. "He's so gorgeous."

"Dove, who is *he*?" Maddy demanded.

"Bob. Bob Anderson." Flinging herself back down on the bed, she told her enchanted audience every word and nuance. "Can you imagine?" she said breathlessly. "He thinks I'm fiery. That's almost like sexy, isn't it?"

Ann nodded and smothered a smile as she listened to the excitement in her daughter's voice. Was this the same child who talked to Reverend Honeycutt earlier in the day? Who became ethereal as she recalled the healing service? Perhaps they had misread Dove this morning. Could their imaginations have been overworked?

"What do you think, Mom? Maddy? About Bob Anderson, that is."

At least this would take her mind off next Tuesday's church service, Ann thought, but deep inside she feared that Dove might be putting too much emphasis on a chance meeting. Oh well, even if it means a transitory heartache later on, distraction right now was welcome.

"Well?" Dove asked anxiously.

Ann's eyes sparkled and she smiled as Maddy swung across the bed and hugged Dove. "Oh, Dove, it's fabulous—I mean—*the* Bob Anderson!" Maddy sat up, her eyes bright. "We should go to the Busy Bee for hamburgers to celebrate when Dad gets home from work. Can we, Mom?"

"Sounds good. It'll give me a night off from cooking."

That night, when the girls were in bed, Ann told Joe about the minister's visit and Dove's response. Then she told him about Bob Anderson. "If she's let down by this boy, she'll be devastated. So much is happening to her all at once."

Joe put his arm around his wife. "You worry too much about her, Ann. It's time she started dating. We'll just have to let nature take its course." He reached for her hand. "If what you say is true, Dove might be in for a big surprise Tuesday night."

"I think she's convinced herself that she had nothing to do with the healing and is out to prove them wrong."

Joe shook his head. "What happened to that simple life we once knew?"

Ann shrugged against his shoulder. "Looks like God had other plans."

"I wish His plans hadn't disrupted our lives like this," Joe said.

The next morning, a sprightly and carefree Dove skipped out of the house before eight, only to return a little after ten, shoulders slumped and head down. She flopped onto a kitchen chair.

"He didn't show, Mom." Tears glistened in her eyes.

Ann pulled up a chair and sat down next to her. What she'd feared was already happening. "He didn't promise he'd be there. Remember? He only asked what beach you go to and said maybe he'd see you." Ann's heart ached for Dove, and she wished she could absorb her hurt.

"But I showed up," Dove said naively.

Ann smiled, patting her daughter's hand. "Girls think differently than boys."

"Well that's dumb."

"But true."

"Do you think he'll be there tomorrow?" Dove's luminescent eyes pleaded for confirmation.

"I wish I could say yes, honey, but I honestly don't know. You know, not even Maddy's life with boys runs smoothly all the time. Remember when Allen went to the mainland last month and forgot he was supposed to take her to the movies?"

Dove shrugged, as if to dismiss the whole incident.

The next three mornings, Dove was at the beach by eight, but Bob didn't show. By the fourth day she'd convinced herself that she'd imagined the whole thing. She'd *wanted* a boy like Bob to say nice things to her. She'd *wanted* him to promise he'd come to the beach to see her. She'd *wanted* to be like the other girls in school and have a boyfriend. She must have wanted this so badly that she put meaning into Bob's words that wasn't really there. Well, she was new at this. She'd learn.

Tuesday night was fast approaching and she had plans to make. She hadn't thought about going back to the Little Church on the Hill because she'd been so wrapped up in dreaming about Bob, but now it was time to face reality, as Maddy would so aptly put it. Dove felt ready. She'd ask her Mom and Dad to sit next to her, knowing they'd do just about anything she might ask for that night.

Once again events were taken out of Dove's hands. Maddy came down with a bad cold, and Ann wouldn't let her attend the service. Dove tried to look and act sorry that Maddy wasn't going to church, but inside she was bursting with joy. Now she could be absolutely, positively sure of the night's outcome.

Ann was immediately on guard when she saw the crowd gathered in front of the church. As they approached, she heard Dove's name whispered.

"There she is," an elderly woman said softly. "Can't miss that red hair."

"Where? Where?" a man asked, pushing forward.

"Just think," the old woman continued, "Catalina's going to be another Lourdes or Fátima."

"She doesn't look very holy to me," another voice exclaimed.

Dove seemed oblivious to the comments of the people milling about, but Ann was worried.

Joe led them down the center aisle to one of the few empty pews left. He motioned Ann into the pew first and then he followed. Dove entered last, leaving enough room for another person to sit next to her.

The little church was filled to capacity with at least ten times the number of people who had attended last week's service. People were crowding into the pews.

"Where is she?" someone whispered. Heads began to turn until they settled on Dove.

In spite of the crowd and the whispering, Dove felt calm. God wasn't going to let her down. Eyes glowing with confidence, she glanced at her father and then reached in front of him to grasp her mother's hand, rewarding her with a smile. "It's okay, Mom."

The soft hum of voices that filled the church abruptly stopped when Reverend Honeycutt entered from the back. On his right was Mr. Brinkley, a deaf white-haired man who'd live on the island for as long as Dove could remember. They stopped at Dove's pew, and Mr. Brinkley sat down next to her and he gave her the kindly smile she knew so well. Dove smiled in return. Reverend Honeycutt walked to the pulpit. A few seconds later when she was sure Mr. Brinkley wasn't watching her, she glanced over at him. She knew he was so deaf he couldn't hear a thing and had to read lips.

"Good evening, everyone and welcome," Reverend

Honeycutt said, interrupting her thoughts. "Tonight we will do a healing of memories."

Letting her mind wander during the opening hymns, Dove thought about lucky Maddy at home who didn't have to listen to Reverend Honeycutt. But Maddy probably would like this sort of stuff, she thought wryly. Then her mind drifted to Bob, but she quickly dismissed him to move back to Maddy again, snug in her bed. She tried everything she could think of to make the time go by faster so she wouldn't have to listen to Reverend Honeycutt—she even checked out the different hair styles of the ladies in front of her—anything so she could get out of the church and back home to her nice, normal life.

Reverend Honeycutt's voice thundered into her consciousness. "Dear friends in Christ, I'd like you to relax—place your feet flat on the floor, and your hands on your lap. Then close your eyes, shutting out everything except my voice." After the shuffling died down, he continued. "I'm going to take you back to when you were an embryo in your mother's womb—very tiny, contented, and warm. Feel this contentment and warmth flowing over and around you. . . ."

This is sick, Dove thought. She glanced quickly at her mother, whose eyes were closed. Dove certainly didn't intend to listen to such dumb stuff.

She succeeded in blocking out Reverend Honeycutt's senseless words for several minutes. Then, like an alarm going off in her head, she heard him announce, "We will now stand and sing the Lord's Prayer as we hold our neighbor's hand."

Suddenly her mind began to reel. Suppose Mr. Brinkley got healed. Impossible, she told herself. He'd been stone deaf forever it seemed—not even a hearing aid helped. Something about flying when he had an inner-ear infection.

She remembered when she'd been younger, in the third or fourth grade, some of the boys used to walk up behind him and yell and clap to see if he was faking. When he didn't respond, they'd jump out at him to scare him. But

Mr. Brinkley was a nice man and never hollered at the kids. He'd just smile kindly and ruffle their hair. When the boys realized they couldn't get a rise out of the old man, they stopped their pranks.

Holding on to those thoughts, Dove reassured herself that nothing she'd be asked to do tonight would change the fact that Mr. Brinkley was deaf.

The strain of the organ recalled her. Suddenly Dove felt the familiar stirring of fear building inside her. She put her hands up to her mouth and shrank back into the pew as her certainty began to waver. Out of the corner of her eye, she saw her mother change places with her father. She was glad to have her closer. She grasped her mother's hand, and held it tightly.

But as soon as she heard the organist begin the introduction to the Lord's Prayer, Dove felt a glowing warmth flow through her. She was instantly at peace; a quiet serenity overtook her. Everything seemed to be happening in slow motion, and she felt as if she were somewhere else, watching from a distance.

Mr. Brinkley took her hand in his, squeezing it gently as they rose for the hymn.

Immediately an intense heat rushed to her hand. Dove knew he felt it too by the way he turned to her with an almost shocked expression on his wrinkled face. Suddenly he took her hands in his and held them over his ears. Dove felt lightheaded and swayed slightly. She thought she was about to faint again.

Abruptly Mr. Brinkley moved her aside and cupped his hands tightly over his ears while moaning loudly. Dove fell back against her mother, who steadied her. They both stared at him.

Everything stopped—the organ playing, the singing voices—everything but Mr. Brinkley's moans. The entire congregation gazed at him. Reverend Honeycutt was by the old man's side in several long strides, asking him what had happened. But something seemed to have dulled Mr. Brinkley's senses. He stared straight ahead, not even bothering to try to read the minister's lips. When he finally glanced up and saw Reverend Honeycutt standing in front of him, he grabbed the minister's shirt and said in a high pitched voice: "I have this ringing sensation in my ears—like a thousand church bells inside my head."

Suddenly the quiet congregation came to life. Murmurings could be heard from all over the church.

"Do you hear that?" a woman's voice exclaimed. "He can hear."

"Don't get carried away now," the man next to her said. "Ringing in the ears is not the same as hearing."

"But . . ."

"Shush," he ordered.

"This isn't what I expected," a voice whined.

"Then go to Lourdes," someone shouted angrily.

The minister looked from the people beginning to mill around to Mr. Brinkley and then to Dove. The strain from the turn of events was evident on her drawn face, and her usually light blue eyes were dark with worry.

Stunned, Dove stood frozen in the pew. What did this mean? Why was Mr. Brinkley hearing bells when he couldn't hear? Was everyone crazy who came to these healing services? Maybe they needed their heads healed instead of their bodies. She shuddered. "I want to go home."

"I think that's good idea," Joe said, taking Ann by the arm.

Ann held Dove's hand tightly and looked again at Mr. Brinkley, who had slumped back into the pew, his head in his hands. He didn't seem to be in pain—he seemed to be in a trance—as if he didn't know where he was. Maybe this whole thing was just too much for the poor old man, she thought as Joe tugged at her arm and led the way through the throng of curious people now crowding the aisles.

Dove glanced at Mr. Brinkley rocking back and forth, still holding his head in his hands. Ashen faced, she turned and walked between her parents.

As they hurried down the aisle and neared the back of the church, Dove spotted Bob Anderson standing near the door next to a pretty girl with long blond hair. When she walked by, he reached out to her, but Dove turned away, sudden tears blurring her vision. So he came to see the show too. Was that girl the reason he didn't show up at the beach?

Oh, what did she care anyway? So he wasn't any better than the rest of the nosy people. Big deal! He wasn't the only boy in Avalon. No, but he was the only one she liked. *Used to like*, she corrected. Then why this aching, empty feeling at the pit of her stomach? Why this enormous sense of disappointment? And why these stupid tears? she asked silently, swiping them away.

The short drive home was made in silence. She hoped her parents thought her tears were for Mr. Brinkley.

Back at the house, they filed into the living room, and Ann switched on the fan. Dove slumped onto the couch, stretching her long legs out in front of her, looking glumly at her big shoes. What a jerk she was—tall, gangly, big feet and hands—a great giant-sized nothing. And dumb to boot, thinking someone like Bob Anderson would consider her special. That blond girl who'd been next to him was more his style. But it hurt too much to think about, so she switched to Mr. Brinkley and his ringing ears. Weird, but at least he wasn't healed.

"I'll go to check on Maddy," Joe said. When he returned, announcing she was fast asleep, Dove took the opportunity to say what was on her mind.

Pushing her hair behind her ears, she sat up. "I'm sorry Mr. Brinkley's ears are ringing, but I'm not sorry he didn't get healed. I know that sounds terrible, but that's how I feel," she said defiantly, still angry at Bob's unexpected presence in church.

"It's always best to be honest, Dove. When our feelings are out in the open, we're better able to handle them."

Dove sighed. Did Mom always have to preach like that? She didn't want to handle her feelings, or anything else for that matter. She just wanted to let her parents know how she felt. Well, now they did.

"Why do you think his ears were ringing?" Joe asked.

"Who knows?" Ann answered testily, then added more calmly, "I've heard it said that some deaf people hear a constant ringing."

"But why now? He didn't have it before," he persisted.

"I don't know if anyone has that answer," Ann told him and then spoke softly to Dove. "I was watching you in church and you looked so dreamy, so far away. What were you feeling?"

Dove didn't answer immediately, but twisted her hands nervously. "I—I had that same feeling—you know, that tingly sensation in my hands I told you about before. After they got real hot, that is. Then I felt like I was going to faint. But all of sudden Mr. Brinkley pushed me away and I sort of came back."

"Came back? Where were you?" Joe asked, instantly alert.

Dove looked puzzled, then stammered, "N—nowhere, actually. I—I just felt like I was. It was like—like watching everything from far away—sort of hazy."

Ann and Joe exchanged glances. That must have been when Dove's face became so beautifully serene, Ann thought. But Mr. Brinkley wasn't healed, so what could it possibly mean?

Before Ann could ask any more questions, Dove cut her off. "Do we have any ice cream, Mom?"

Ann sensed her daughter's reluctance to discuss something she couldn't understand. "Chocolate, vanilla, and strawberry. Take your pick," she said cheerfully and headed for the kitchen.

"Chocolate," Dove answered.

"Ditto," said Joe.

While they ate, Dove talked about some unusual fish she'd seen while snorkeling last week, and Ann let her run on, sensing the child needed time to collect her emotions. After they finished their ice cream, Dove put her spoon down and said sheepishly, "I really do hope Mr. Brinkley's going to be all right." Then she took the stairs two at a time and ran down the hall to her room.

Alone with her thoughts, the realization that she *hadn't* healed Mr. Brinkley finally dawned on Dove, but for some reason she didn't feel as excited as she'd expected to feel. Well, tonight she'd proved to the whole village that she didn't have the gift of healing. A bit of happiness and relief began to surface, and she twirled around and around. Then a sudden, nagging thought came into focus and she plopped down on her bed.

If her touch made Mr. Brinkley's ears ring in such a way that they seemed to bother him, did that mean she had some sort of *evil* power?

Frightened by the thought, she opened her bedroom door just as the phone rang. She heard her mother speaking softly, but couldn't make out what she was saying. As she started down the stairs, her mother's astonished voice reached her. "Are you absolutely sure?"

Intuitively knowing the words had something to do with her, Dove ran back to her room and slammed the door.

Chapter Six

Huddled in bed, Dove stared at the door, waiting for the ominous knock she knew was forthcoming. Maybe Mr. Brinkley died and everyone would blame her. What else could it be? She searched her mind for an answer. Perhaps the ringing in his ears got so bad he went crazy. Dove shuddered and wrapped her arms around her knees, pulling them to her chest.

Terrified at what she might hear, she nonetheless welcomed the soft knock and her mother's voice. "Dove, are you awake?" Without waiting for an answer, Ann opened the door and slipped in. She moved slowly to the bed and sat down, taking Dove's hand in hers.

"He's dead, isn't he?" Dove asked, her blue eyes luminous with unshed tears.

"Dead? Mr. Brinkley?"

Dove nodded, biting down on her lower lip to keep her tears in check.

"Oh, Dove, no. He's not dead. He regained his hearing."

Dove shook her head in denial. It couldn't be true. It just couldn't. Someone must have lied to her mother. "I don't believe it," she whispered.

"The phone call—that was Reverend Honeycutt. He was with Mr. Brinkley at his house, and he said he felt completely helpless as he listened to the poor man constantly talk about the ringing sensation in his ears. Then all of a sudden Mr. Brinkley stood up and looked around him, a puzzled expression on his face. The ringing had quit, he told Reverend Honeycutt. When the Reverend murmured, 'thank God,' Mr. Brinkley, who was facing the other way, answered, 'Amen.' Then the two men turned to each other at the same time, and Mr. Brinkley cried out, 'The Lord has heard my prayers. I can hear again.' " Ann looked at her daughter, and her heart ached at the sight of Dove's stricken face. "That's word for word what Reverend Honeycutt told me."

Dove continued shaking her head in silent denial.

"I don't know what to say, Dove. This gift that God has given you . . ."

"I don't want His gift," she shouted, glaring at her mother.

Ann remained calm. "What is, is. It's not going to do you any good to keep fighting it." Even though she wasn't getting through to her daughter, Ann took a deep breath and continued, "I don't know what to think. I've been at church with you twice and I saw what happened, but I don't understand it." She took Dove's face in her hands. "I watched you tonight, honey. You change somehow. You become serene and angelic-looking."

Dove furiously shook her head.

"Oh, I know I sound melodramatic," Ann continued, "but I don't know how else to explain the change that comes over you."

"I wasn't feeling good. Maybe I'm getting Maddy's cold. I probably got pale because I was going to faint again right there in church." Her eyes pleaded for acceptance of her words.

Ann caressed the coppery hair and said softly, "Perhaps. But honey, you're not the fainting type—you never have been." She straightened up and said quietly, "In any event, Reverend Honeycutt wants to come over tomorrow to talk to you. . . ."

"No." Dove shot up in bed, her face livid with rage.

"I'm not going to talk to him and I'm *never* setting foot inside that church again. *Never!*"

"I know it's been a traumatic night. . . ."

"You don't know the worst of it." She leaped off the bed and hurled the words in fury.

"What do you mean?"

She spun around, her face crimson with indignation. "Bob Anderson, that's what. He was at church tonight." She forced the lump from her throat. "I thought he—he liked me, but he just wanted to be nosy—like the rest of those horrible people." She crumpled on the bed, tears coming in a rush.

"Oh, honey, I'm sure he wasn't being nosy," Ann said, feeling Dove's heartache even as she caressed her hair. "He probably attends church regularly."

"Well, he never showed up at the beach, but he sure as heck showed up at church, just watching and waiting to see what happened. You know. Like when you watch a three-ring circus. That's me, all right. Dove Sanders—circus star."

Ann ignored the all too familiar complaint and took Dove's hand, trying not to look down at what was probably a miraculous vessel. "Did he speak to you?"

"No." She jerked upright and with a swish of her hand, wiped away her tears. Her head rose defiantly. "He put his hand out, but I just ignored him. Besides, he had a girl with him." Suddenly, her anger dissolved and she fell dejectedly on the bed. "Why is all this happening, Mom? Why? Did I do something wrong? Is God punishing me?"

"Oh, Dove, baby, no, no." Ann took her daughter in her arms. "God doesn't punish. It's just that sometimes we don't understand His ways. And because we don't understand, we have a tendency to fight Him." Like you're doing, Ann thought. "If we're able to, it's best just to remain calm and let things happen naturally."

"You mean I should stop fighting this healing thing?"

Ann nodded. "If you've been blessed with the gift of healing, there's nothing you can do about it. If you *don't* have it, things will simply quiet down on their own and eventually people will forget any of this ever happened."

Dove listened to her mother, but she had her own ideas. She knew she would never give in.

"Do you understand, Dove?" Dove nodded, but Ann was aware her daughter hadn't looked her in the eye. Sighing, she rose and pulled back the sheet. "Get some sleep," she said gently and kissed her daughter good night. "We'll talk about this tomorrow, okay?"

But Dove turned her head away and didn't answer. When she heard her mother close the door, she covered her face with the pillow and wept.

"I hate it! I hate it! I hate it!" Although muffled by the pillow Dove pressed against her face, the words screamed inside her head. She pounded her fists into an old teddy bear, wanting to tear the stuffing out of the casing, to somehow hurt the lifeless object the way she was hurting.

Flinging it aside, she brought her hands slowly in front of her face and splayed her fingers, tears of frustration streaming from her eyes. "Why did you go and do this to me, God?" she cried out in anguish. "Why?"

Clenching her fists against her rigid body, she glared at the soft pink ceiling and the tiny silver stars shining down on her. "Well, let me tell You something. I don't want this—this *gift*. Do you hear me, God? I don't want it. And You can't make me use it. I don't care what anyone says. You can't make me."

A couple of minutes later, Maddy opened Dove's door and poked her head in. Sniffling, she asked: "What happened at church? I tried to stay awake, reading, but it didn't work." She grabbed a tissue from the box on the night table and sneezed.

"It turned out horrible," Dove exploded, kicking the sheet off. She repeated the story about Mr. Brinkley, but stopped abruptly when she came to the part about seeing Bob and the girl in the back of the church.

"Isn't it wonderful that Mr. Brinkley's healed?" Maddy exclaimed.

"You're sick, Maddy," Dove said disgustedly, yanking the sheet back up. "Mr. Brinkley was getting along just fine when he couldn't hear. So what's so wonderful?"

"Dove!" Maddy was clearly horrified as she plopped down on the bed. "You can't mean that! God has given you a beautiful gift and you talk about it like it was something ugly."

"To me it's ugly. Because I don't want any part of it. And that goes for talking about it, too. As far as I'm concerned, none of this stuff ever happened."

"But think of the people you can help. You can go to the churches and hospitals and retirement homes. . . ."

Dove shook her head, wondering what planet her sister came from. "Look, Maddy. Why God went ahead and did such a dumb thing, I don't know, but I'm not going to any churches or hospitals so people can stare at me like I was some kind of religious fanatic. And from now on, I never want to talk about it again. Never."

"But you can't ignore . . ."

Her temper rising, Dove glared at her twin, grabbing her wrist. "Can't I? You just wait and see."

Maddy pulled her hand away. "Okay, so what else happened that you're keeping back?"

Dove started to pretend ignorance, but she knew her twin's intuition; Maddy would keep on till she got it out of her. Taking a deep breath to steady her voice, she said: "I saw Bob at church. You know, Maddy, he was the last person in the world I wanted to see there. The *very last*. And there was a girl with him. I sure had him pegged all wrong," she said, chewing on her bottom lip to keep it from trembling. "He came to gape at me just like the rest of the village."

Maddy said, "How do you know he was with a girl? The church was crowded, wasn't it? And what makes you think he was there gaping? Couldn't he have just been interested in what happened to you?"

Dove shrugged. "He wasn't interested enough in me to come to the beach. He was probably tied up with *her*."

Maddy sneezed again and returned to the main point. "You were glad I couldn't go to church tonight, weren't you?"

Dove actually gasped, she was so surprised. "How in the world did you know that? Oh yes, you and your *intuition*." Dove shrugged in resignation. "I thought it was you who had the healing power and if you weren't in church nothing would happen."

"If there was any way I could take it from you, I would gladly," Maddy said.

Dove nodded. "I know." Then she looked pleadingly at Maddy sprawled on the foot of her bed. "Do I have to go back again next week—to church, I mean?"

Maddy's expression was serene. "That's up to you. You must do what you feel is right, what's comfortable for you."

"And what if the two aren't the same? I mean, supposing I think something's right, but I know it'll make me uncomfortable. What do I do then?" Dove persisted.

"Pray about it."

Annoyed, Dove sat bolt upright. "That's your answer for everything, isn't it?"

"It's everyone's answer for everything." Maddy rose and hugged her sister. "Good night, Dove. Please don't be unhappy. Remember—we all love you. Especially God."

When Maddy left, Dove flopped back against the pillow and stared up at the ceiling, wishing herself somewhere else for the first time in her short life. But she didn't have the option of running away. Where could she run to on an island?

Paloma suddenly jumped up on the bed, and Dove snuggled her into the curve of her young body. Exhausted by the emotions churning inside, she soon fell asleep.

The next morning, Dove decided to go to the beach early to be alone and to think. Deep inside, though, she hoped Bob would be there—alone. She had to know if he was her friend or not and somehow find out who that girl was. Munching on a cinnamon bun she'd grabbed from the cupboard, she dashed out the front door, hurrying toward the beach. It would have been quicker if she had taken the bike, but her mother was probably out back in the garden and Dove didn't want to chance it. She wasn't ready to face her just yet.

If Bob had heard about Mr. Brinkley—and she was sure all of Avalon had by this time—maybe he'd be at the beach waiting for her. Perhaps he *had* been at the church because he was interested, as Maddy suggested. More than anything in the world Dove wanted to believe that.

As she approached Front Street, she scanned the beach and saw Bob sitting on the sand, his back against a palm tree. Alone. Dove stopped and called to him.

He smiled and patted a place on the sand next to him, then moved over so she could lean back, too. They were quiet for a long time, and without looking at him, she said, "I guess you heard about Mr. Brinkley."

Bob murmured something that sounded like an agreement.

"Nothing's changed. I mean, I still don't want it." She looked at him sideways and waited. When he didn't answer, she said, "Well, aren't you going to say anything?"

His deep blue eyes met hers. It occurred to her they were very honest eyes. "What do you want me to say? That you're right?" She nodded almost imperceptibly. "I don't have the answer, Dove. If you don't want this gift, you must have a reason. But you have to decide what's right for you." When she said nothing, he added softly, "Dove, it's between you and God."

"I thought you were going to be my friend," she said sulkily.

"I am your friend. But no one can make this decision for you. Not even your parents or your sister."

"I'm tired of being the town freak," she said, writing in the sand with her finger.

"There's nothing freaky about you, Dove."

She looked away shyly. "What would you do if God had given it to you?"

Bob shook his head slowly. "That's a hard question to answer. I would be honored, but truthfully I'm not good enough for such a gift."

"Neither am I. Do you think He made a mistake? That He meant it for Maddy?" she asked seriously.

He touched her hand. "God doesn't make mistakes."

"Well, I think He did this time. Let's walk," she suggested suddenly. They rose and walked silently a moment, their feet squishing in the damp sand.

"What does your family think?" Bob asked after a while.

Dove hesitated, unwilling to talk more about it. But finally she shrugged. "I'm not sure. Of course, Maddy thinks it's the greatest thing that ever happened. But Maddy's like that—religious, I mean. I haven't talked to my dad yet, but he and Mom are worried. They think I'm going to pieces over this." She stopped walking and waited till Bob paused and turned to her. "I told Maddy I don't intend to discuss it with anyone—ever. And I meant that."

He gave a slow smile. "But we're talking about it. . . ."

They began walking again, close to the water, letting it gently lap at their feet. "I know. But somehow you're different. You don't try to push me into doing something I don't want to do. Like families do." Suddenly Dove stopped. "Bob," she said earnestly, "if I don't use this gift, will you still like me? I mean as a friend?" she added quickly.

He smiled at her shyly. "I liked you before you got it—when I saw you at school."

"But you didn't show up at the beach. . . ."

"I wanted to. But I had to go to San Diego with my mother to pick up my cousin Sue."

"You did?" she asked, suddenly beaming and feeling all cozy inside. So that's who the blonde was. His cousin!

"I really did," he said. She liked his shy smile.

For the first time in what seemed like years to her, Dove was happy—a nice bubbly kind of joy that spread all

through her like warm chocolate pudding. "I think I'd
better get home now," she said, not really wanting to
leave but knowing she should. "My mom's probably wondering what happened to me."

"Wait." Bob scratched the side of his face nervously.
"I've never told this to anyone, but it's something I'd like
to tell you. I know you'll understand."

Don't tell me you're moving to San Diego, Dove thought
in anguish. Anything but that! She looked at him appre-
hensively, her fingers crossed behind her back.

"You see," he continued, "I think I want to be a
minister. No, that's not true. I'm *sure* I want to be a
minister." He waited as if measuring her reaction and then
went on. "It's like this: There are so many people out
there running around in circles and maybe—just maybe—
I'll be able to touch some lives and—and help them in
some way." He shook his head. "I'm not even sure
how."

He gave her a nervous smile that made her feel
protective of him. Then she asked curiously, "But I don't
get it. Why can't you tell anyone?"

"They'd laugh at me, especially my parents," he said,
looking down at his feet. "My family's not very religious
—I'm the only one who goes to church. They wouldn't
understand—they'd make a big joke out of it."

Suddenly Dove felt very close to Bob. She knew exactly
how he felt. In her case, it wasn't her family who'd made
a joke out of her situation, it was everyone else. But no
matter who laughs, it hurts. She guessed it would be
worse, though, if it were family.

Then a frightening thought came to mind, and her heart
sank to her knees. Was this healing thing the only reason
he was interested in her? Because it fit in with his idea of
ministers and helping people and stuff like that? She hoped
not. No! Didn't he say the first time they talked that he
thought she was different—fiery? For as long as she lived
she'd remember that word. *Fiery.*

"You have a nice family, Dove," Bob continued. "They stick by you. I saw your mom and dad at church and could tell they were concerned for you." They began walking again. "I don't have that with my parents. They kind of do their own thing. They buy me things and feed and clothe me, but we never really talk. I think more than anything I'd like to feel close to my mom and dad. It gets kind of lonely with no one to talk to."

"Maybe you should see Reverend Honeycutt," Dove suggested. "I bet he'd understand. And it would help take his mind off me," she added, trying to lighten his mood.

Bob laughed, but his blue eyes remained serious. "You really don't want anything to do with healing, do you? You know, I wish something like that would happen to me."

"You're kidding!"

"No. I'm dead serious. I think a person who is given a gift like that has to be special in God's eyes. You must be special to Him. . . ."

Dove stopped walking and stood with her hands on her hips, her eyes shooting sparks of anger at Bob. "Let's get something straight right now, Bob. I am *not* special in God's eyes. Furthermore, I do not *want* His gift of healing nor will I *accept* it. And I'm not going to talk about this healing stuff anymore, not even with you." She started to walk away, head high and shoulders squared.

He caught up with her and touched her arm. "Hey, I'm sorry. It's just hard for me to figure out why you're reacting so negatively to something so positive."

Dove looked at him and shook her head slowly. "Why is it no one seems to understand—not my family—not Reverend Honeycutt—and not even you. I just want to be normal. That's all." With a catch in her voice, she whispered, "Is that too much to ask of God?"

Bob must have heard the anguish in her voice because he grabbed a strand of her hair and tugged it. "Come on. Let's rent some gear and go snorkeling. I'll race you to the pier," he said before breaking into a run. Grateful, she sprinted after him.

After returning the snorkeling equipment an hour later, they plopped down, settling themselves in the shade of a fat palm tree. Bob looked thoughtful. "Now that I've told you my secret, what do you want to do when you get out of school?" he asked, picking up a piece of driftwood and tracing ticktacktoe squares in the sand.

"Oh, I want to own my own snorkeling business and live on Catalina forever." Deep down inside, she also wanted to get married, have four kids, and two cats. But she couldn't tell him that!

"Wouldn't you ever want to leave the island? Live somewhere else in California? There's a whole other world out there."

"I don't think so," she mused. "Unless my mom and dad and Maddy came too."

Bob studied her pensively. "It must be nice to feel that way about your family. You're very close to your sister, aren't you?"

"Of course. She's my twin."

"She *is*? You sure don't look alike. I wondered why you were both in the same grade."

Suddenly feeling all arms and legs, Dove looked away, wishing with all her heart that she was beautiful. "I know," she said, trying not to let any bitterness show through. "She's small and pretty and I'm big and plain."

Bob's hearty laugh startled her. "Do you need glasses?"

"What do you mean?"

"There's nothing plain about you! In a couple of years you're going to have every guy on the island after you." Then he said shyly, looking away as though embarrassed, "You're gonna be a real beauty with that red hair and those blue eyes of yours."

Dove felt herself blushing and knew her face was every bit as red as the hair on her head. She was glad Bob wasn't looking at her. But his words sang in her heart. A real beauty, he'd said. Nobody had ever used those words to describe Dove Sanders. A real beauty—and fiery. Wow!

She heard the chimes tower tolling nine o'clock. "Got to go now," she said quietly.

He took her hand to help her up, and Dove felt a warmth creep into her fingers, but it was different from the warmth she'd felt at church. Her mind raced through all sorts of romantic dreams—dancing with Bob at the prom—kissing—dating—getting married—having kids. She began to laugh. Now she was really crazy. Marriage was years away. Right now Bob thought she was fiery and was going to be a real beauty. That was enough. That was more than enough.

"I'll walk you as far as the bank," Bob told her. "My dad wants me to do some errands for him." At the bank they said good-bye and Dove kept on going.

Some of the shops on Front Street were opening, and Dove waved to the owners as she hurried by. Was it her imagination, or were they looking at her with a strange light in their eyes? Then, in a matter of minutes, the pleasant time shared with Bob was wiped out of her mind. She heard the whispering.

"Poor thing. Pretending nothing happened . . ."

"Hard to believe that gangly girl has the power . . ."

"Mass hysteria. That's what it is . . ."

Someone turned on a radio and the song "Everyone's Gone to the Moon" drifted out onto the street. She'd give anything to be able to go to the moon right now, she thought. Anywhere to get away from prying eyes and questioning lips.

Dove knew she had to do something, but she wasn't sure what that something was. One thing was certain—she couldn't just sit back and let things happen. And she couldn't discuss it anymore with her family—it was too painful. She couldn't talk to Bob about it either, because this so-called gift was something he'd give anything to have, and there she was, wanting to be rid of it.

Maddy had said she should talk to God. So had Bob, for

that matter. Dove mulled this over as she crossed Sumner Avenue, vaguely aware of the activity going on in the cluster of summer houses she passed.

God didn't seem very eager to get her out of this mess, she thought. Heavy-hearted, Dove walked back to her house.

Chapter Seven

"Hi," *her* mother greeted her at the door. "Been to the beach?"

Dove nodded.

"How about some breakfast?" Ann asked, moving to the refrigerator. "What would you like? Eggs? French toast?" Food had a way of perking Dove up.

"Both. All of a sudden I'm starving." She felt better, now that she was back at home. With good food in the making, all thoughts of healing and God's apparent unwillingness to help her were set aside. "Where's Maddy?"

"In her room."

Dove poured a glass of milk while her mother placed the eggs and French toast on the table. Sipping her coffee, Ann waited for Dove to finish eating, then said, "Reverend Honeycutt called this morning. . . ."

Her peaceful feeling vanished, and her voice was firm. "I won't go, Mom, so please don't ask me. I don't want to have anything to do with this healing stuff. And I don't want to talk about it anymore. Not with Reverend Honeycutt —not with anyone. If I don't go to the service, then I can't heal anyone. Then everyone will forget it ever happened," she said in a rush. "That's what I want—to forget it ever happened."

Ann nodded. "Okay, honey, I'll tell him."

Something in her mother's quiet acceptance bothered Dove. She wanted to ignore it, yet she couldn't. "Mom, are you disappointed in me?"

Ann reached across the table and placed her hand over Dove's. "No, honey, I've never been disappointed in you. I'm just sorry that this has become such a burden to you."

"It'll go away, Mom. You'll see." She fought back tears, touched by her mother's concern. "It just has to. It has to," she cried.

Ann walked around the table to Dove and held her tightly, smoothing her hair, burnished by the sunlight streaming through the window. "Don't worry, love. No matter what happens, everything will be all right. Somehow we'll make it all right. With all of us working together, we can't lose."

Dove nodded her head, encouraged by her mother's words. She had never failed her yet.

Dinner that night was strained, not at all like their usually informal meals. Afraid that someone in her family might bring up Mr. Brinkley's healing, Dove chattered away about meeting Bob on the beach and the new glass-bottom boat service scheduled to take snorkelers out for an hour. Suddenly she realized her throat ached from talking so much and was relieved when Maddy excused herself. Taking the opportunity, she rose from the table too.

When her parents exchanged glances, Dove saw a look of hopelessness in their expressions. Suddenly she wanted to stamp her feet and yell at the top of her lungs for them to forget about it—to stop making it into such a big deal. She wanted to run away to some far off place, to disappear. Instead she walked calmly up the stairs with Maddy. In order not to upset her family, she had to push her own feelings down inside her.

Maddy said she wanted to get away so she could talk to Dove.

"What do you want to talk about?" Dove asked.

"What families are all about. About you and me as

sisters—twins—friends. And how we can help you if you'll only let us."

Dove bristled and the hair on the back of her neck stood on end. "Don't you listen to anything I say anymore? I don't need any help. I just need to be left alone. Why can't we talk about snorkeling or swimming or your stained glass? Why do we always have to talk about—about healing? I'm sick to death of that subject. I would think you'd be too."

Maddy put her hand on Dove's arm. "I'm sorry I always seem to be upsetting you lately, but it—it's such a beautiful . . ."

"To you maybe, but to me it's ugly." She shook Maddy's hand off her arm.

"I say beautiful." Smiling impishly, Maddy kissed Dove on the cheek and ran out of the room.

Dove stared at the closed door.

Cheeks flushed, Dove plopped down on the bed. "Paloma, where are you?" She looked around for her kitten. "What a life!" she exclaimed, dragging the white ball of fur over to her. "All you do is sleep. That scratching post and toys sure must tire you out." Looking into blue eyes that mirrored her own, Dove suggested, "Do you think we could change places? I certainly wouldn't mind spending my days sleeping. No, huh? Well then let's go sit on the balcony." Snuggling the kitten to her chest, she went out and sat down on the old-fashioned rocking chair.

"What is this?" she said, removing a book from under her. She held it up. A Bible. Just looking at it made her angry. Why couldn't they leave her alone? "Maddy must have left it. That girl never gives up, does she?" She placed it on the small table next to the rocker. Stroking the purring kitten, she watched the sky turn from a soft pink into a flaming red and felt the anger drain slowly out of her. Yet a restlessness remained. When the first star appeared, she quickly made a wish and then went back inside.

Paloma found her crocheted ball and began batting it around, catching her sharp little claws in the yarn and rolling over and over, trying to disengage it. Dove watched her in amusement for a few minutes, but she still felt the unaccustomed restlessness. She began pacing the small room.

She walked out on the balcony again, and her gaze fell on the Bible. Slowly she picked it up and leafed through it. What was it she'd read some place? If you want an answer to a problem, take the Bible, open it at random, and your gaze will fall on the answer.

It was worth a try. Dove carried the Bible back into her room, turned on the bedside light, and opened the Holy Book. Sitting down, she read from Matthew: "But when you pray, go to your private room and, when you have shut your door, pray to your Father who is in that secret place, and your Father who sees all that is done in secret will reward you."

Dove closed the Bible and lay diagonally across the bed thinking about the passage.

Suddenly she jumped up from the bed, her face alight. "Okay, God," she said aloud, "here goes. Maddy told me to pray to You, Bob told me to talk to You, and the gospel according to Matthew just told me the same thing. Everyone seems to think that this healing business is between You and me.

"You gave it to me without asking first, and that wasn't fair," she said as she clutched the closed Bible to her chest and paced the room. "Maybe You thought it would make me happy, but it didn't. To be honest, it made me miserable. I hope I don't hurt Your feelings, God, but I don't want this gift. I'm not made for all this holy stuff. It just isn't me. I thought You knew that. . . ."

Falling to her knees at the side of the bed, Dove placed the Bible on the spread and buried her face in her hands. "I don't mean to sound like a smart aleck, God, and really I'm not. But please, I beg You, please take back this—this gift. I'll do anything else You ask me. Anything. But not this, God. Please, not this."

She didn't feel as if she'd reached Him. Maybe she could make a bargain with Him. "If You take it back, I'll go to church every Sunday. I'll read the Bible every night before I go to sleep. And I'll be good to my mother; I won't answer her back or talk fresh. I promise, God. And I'll never ever complain about my frizzy hair and yucky eyes and big feet and hands. But please, just take it back."

Leaning on the bed, Dove's hand touched the Bible and she reached for it. As she sat on the floor and opened it, she knew somehow that she would find her answer. She leafed through several pages and stopped once again at Matthew. Looking down, she read: "Whatever you ask in prayer, you will receive, if you have faith."

Scrambling to her feet, Dove clasped the Bible to her breast and chanted aloud. "I knew You'd help me, God. I knew it—I knew it—I knew it."

For the first time in weeks, except for those moments at church, Dove felt completely at peace—a nice soothing tranquillity that wrapped around her like a warm blanket. She undressed and got into bed, and fell asleep almost instantly.

When she awoke the next morning, she felt as though a thousand pounds had been taken from her shoulders. But she also realized that although *she* knew God had taken back the gift, no one else did. And as long as they didn't know the truth, they would look upon her as someone different—the weird kid with healing hands. She'd have to prove to Reverend Honeycutt and the congregation—yes, and to her family—that she was just plain Dove Sanders. And that meant going to another healing service. The very thought made her shudder, but she knew she had to do it. Only one more time, she kept telling herself. Only one more time. And alone. No family. She wanted to do it alone.

She had to talk to Bob. He'd help her do it.

Ann didn't question Dove when she announced she was taking a walk to the beach. These early morning visits seemed to be helping her.

Half skipping, half running, Dove arrived at Crescent Beach only to find it empty. Oh, there were dozens of beach towels laid out with books and suntan lotion strewn over them, but it was too early yet for the tourists. The Avalon residents laughed at this daily routine. Beach towels would miraculously appear on the sand before the sun even had a chance to rise, but the tourists didn't show up till nine or ten.

Too nervous to sit and wait, Dove took off her shoes and waded in the shallow water while scanning the streets leading to the beach, watching for Bob. He had to show up today. He just had to. She didn't think she could keep this news to herself another day. Maybe she could stop by the bank and ask his father to tell him to come by her house. No, that was being too forward, she decided. Besides, she was too shy.

Just when she was about to give up and go home, Bob came running down the beach. She dashed up to meet him.

"I had a feeling you'd be here waiting," he said, smiling at her.

"Bob, come and sit down." She grabbed his hand. "I have something really great to tell you. I mean—*really* great!"

They sat on the low wall, their feet in the damp sand, and Dove told him everything that had happened to her the previous night.

"But Dove, it could have been a coincidence that you picked out those particular passages to read. It doesn't have to be a sign from God," he said cautiously, as if trying not to break her bubble.

"But it was A sign from God, I mean. Bob, listen," she said, grabbing his arm. "I felt it in my heart. Oh, I know. I'm sounding like Maddy now. But it's true— everything I told you and knew in my heart and felt deep inside—is true. I prayed and God answered."

Bob shook his head slowly as if trying to absorb everything she was telling him. She wondered why he seemed so doubtful. He was the one who was religious. He should know God would send her a message through the Bible. God did things like that, as Reverend Honeycutt and Maddy were always saying.

"I need you to do me a favor," she said.

"What kind of favor?"

"I want to go to the healing service next week, but I don't want my family to know. I'd like you to go with me."

"How are you going to get out of the house without their knowing?"

Biting down on her lip, she sighed. "I thought I'd tell them I was going to the movies with you and your parents."

"I'd do almost anything for you, Dove, but don't ask me to be part of a lie to your parents. How would I ever face them?"

She looked defeated.

"Besides, I really don't understand. Why can't you tell them?"

She sighed. Why did he have to be so conscientious? Yet she knew that's what she liked about him. "Everything's changed at my house since this happened. My parents keep looking at each other funny. Maddy walks around as if I'm some sort of saint. I want to do it all by myself and then tell them—when it's all over. If they go with me, they'll be expecting something a lot different from what's going to happen."

"Not if you tell them about last night."

"Bob, you're my friend and *you* don't really believe God took back His gift. Now be honest. Do you?"

He averted his gaze. "I—I'm not sure"

"There! So what are *they* going to think? The same thing you do. That there's going to be some sort of healing and I'll fall to pieces." Her blue eyes pleaded, "Honest, it'll be much better my way."

"I don't see it like that, Dove. I'm afraid you'll either have to tell your parents or go by yourself."

She grabbed her sneakers and glared angrily at him, then rose and strode off down the beach. Why couldn't he help her out? Just this once. She'd never asked him to do anything for her before. He was acting like some goody-two-shoes. He thinks just like Maddy. Everything has to be on the up and up. Darn! At the corner, she turned around to see if he was following her, but he was gone. She put her sneakers on and took the long way home.

As her anger dissolved, she began to think about what Bob had said. Was he right? Should she tell her parents? She didn't know what to do. Oh well, there were still five days before the service. Plenty of time to resolve the matter.

Dove stayed away from the beach for the next couple of days so she could make her decision without Bob's influence—at least that's what she tried to tell herself. The real reason was that she was still upset with Bob for letting her down, and she wanted to punish him. She doubted, though, that he felt nearly as bad about not seeing her as she did at not seeing him.

On Sunday, her parents and Maddy went to church, but Dove stayed home. She'd stay out of church until after she proved herself at the healing service. Then she'd go to church every Sunday, no matter what. Wasn't that part of her bargain with God?

The ringing of the doorbell startled her. She walked over to the door and opened it.

"Hi. I didn't see you at the beach for a couple of days, so I thought I'd stop by to see what was going on. You weren't sick, were you?" Bob asked.

Happiness welled up inside her. He had actually come to the house to see how she was. "No, I hardly ever get sick," she said. "Come on in. Want a Coke?" He nodded, and she put some ice in glasses and set them on the kitchen table.

"How come you're not at church?" she asked.

"I started to go, but I kept thinking about you. So I decided to come here instead."

Dove's cheeks turned pink with pleasure.

"How's everything going?" he asked, pouring his drink and sitting at the kitchen table.

She sat down across from him and sighed. "You know, it's like doom and gloom around here. I know Reverend Honeycutt keeps calling 'cause I can hear my mom telling him I refuse to talk to him or go near the church. Nobody says anything directly to me—I made sure that stopped days ago—but I can tell that's the only thing on their minds."

"Don't you think you should tell them what happened the other night and let them decide for themselves whether they want to believe it or not?"

Dove sipped her Coke. "I never thought of it that way."

"If you want to tell them you plan on going to the healing service Tuesday night, I'll stay here till they get home, to give you moral support. You know, Dove, it might be a relief for them like it was for you."

"If they believe it. Do you believe it now?" she asked softly, meeting his eyes.

He nodded and said, "I'm sorry I acted like 'doubting Thomas' the other day."

She brightened. "They'll be home soon, and we're going to have brunch. We do that every Sunday—makes the day sort of special. Will you stay? I just might need that support you offered."

"Hey, am I your friend or what?" he answered, smiling.

Dove watched Bob's face change slowly—he looked pensive, almost brooding. She touched his arm. "What's the matter? You look like you lost your best friend."

"Worse. Last night I took my own advice."

"What advice?"

"I talked to my parents. I told them I wasn't going to

follow in my Dad's footsteps and be a banker—that I was going to be a minister.''

Shifting her chair closer, Dove asked, "What did they say? Were they mad?''

"At first they were speechless. They stared at me as if they'd never seen me before. When it sank in, they exchanged glances, and my father muttered something about it being a whim and I would grow out of it.''

"And your mom?''

"She said my choice wasn't a very prestigious career goal and she hoped I'd come to my senses soon.''

Dove's fist banged the table. "Oh, Bob, how unfair! I hate to say it, but they don't sound very nice.''

"Sometimes they're not,'' he said, glancing away

When Dove heard the front door, she suddenly felt giddy. She'd never had a visit from a boy before—never mind introducing one to her parents! Her insides began to tighten in anticipation. All worry about telling them of her talk with God fled in the face of this stupendous task.

The introductions weren't as bad as she'd imagined, and her mom and dad seemed to really like Bob. Maddy did too. But not too much, Dove hoped, fingers crossed for good luck.

With everyone in a pleasant mood, it seemed the right time to reveal her pact with God. Maddy, true to form, was absolutely convinced God had talked to her. There was no doubt in Maddy's mind that the gift had been withdrawn. Her belief was contagious, and soon Ann and Joe began talking as if it were definitely gone, and how they looked forward to their lives getting back to normal. Dove was relieved. She silently thanked Bob for setting her straight. Now she wouldn't mind their attending the healing service with her.

Maddy spoke up. "I'm glad you decided to go to the next healing service. I know this is hard for you, but it'll give you strength.''

"What does that mean?''

"It means that by facing this 'thing' as you call it—even though you'd rather forget all about it and get on with your life—you're building character and strength."

"Maddy—you're weird! You sound just like a shrink. I say nuts to character and strength. I'm doing it so people will leave me alone."

Bob, Ann, and Joe chuckled at her bluntness, but Maddy remained serious.

"But someday you might need the strength you're building now," her sister answered softly. "And then you'll have it."

Dove screwed up her face as if she'd sucked a lemon. "Where do you come up with these things? Now you sound like a book. I think you read too much and it's affecting your brain. Don't you agree, Mom?"

Ann ruffled Dove's hair in answer and smiled lovingly at both her daughters.

"Let's not tell Reverend Honeycutt or anyone else that we're going, okay?" Dove said. "The fewer people who know, the better."

"I doubt if he'll ask anymore. I must have told him a dozen times that you refuse to go," Ann said. "I think it's a safe bet that no one will expect you."

After brunch, Bob excused himself, saying he'd better be getting on home.

"Stop by again," Joe said, shaking the young man's hand.

"You're going to church with us Tuesday night, aren't you?" Dove asked as she walked him to the front door. He held her hand, and she wished he'd never let it go.

"I said I would," he whispered in her ear, and Dove felt her knees weaken.

"Come by the house about six-thirty and we'll all go together," she said.

Dove watched him saunter down the street. She was glad he had met her family. Dove had secretly been afraid that once Bob met Maddy, he'd like her better, but he had hardly even looked at her. Almost floating in sheer bliss, Dove returned to the kitchen.

When they arrived at the church Tuesday evening, Ann was relieved to see only a few people sitting on the park benches in the church courtyard. A small group was singing "I Have Decided to Follow Jesus" when Bob and her family entered the sanctuary. This time, they had their choice of pews and took one near the front.

When Reverend Honeycutt saw Dove he looked surprised, but recovered quickly and asked her to come up to the front of the church. Winking impishly at her parents, she followed him.

"I didn't expect you here tonight," he said in a whisper.

"I changed my mind."

"So I see. Do you mind coming up here at the end of the service when we sing the Lord's Prayer? I'd like to have a small group in a circle tonight."

Dove nodded agreement, then returned to the pew and sat down next to Bob. She noticed how intently he listened to the prophecies. He actually looked like he believed all that stuff. It might be his cup of tea, but it sure wasn't hers!

When the organist began playing, Dove joined the people who surrounded Reverend Honeycutt. The young boy in the wheelchair on her left clasped his hand around hers. Dove stiffened, momentarily unsure of what might happen.

She glanced down at the boy, whose eyes shone with hope. Was he expecting a miracle? Suddenly, Dove was afraid.

But Dove felt nothing—absolutely nothing. No warmth, no tingling, no faraway feeling. She realized that even though there were only a few people in the church, every one of them had their eyes riveted on her. Even the boy in the wheelchair. But this would be the last time.

After the Lord's Prayer had been sung, Reverend Honeycutt looked at each person in the congregation. He stepped closer to Dove, puzzlement clearly showing in his expression.

"It's gone, Reverend," Dove said softly. "You see, I asked God to take it back and He did."

Chapter Eight

Dove watched the boy wheel himself down the center aisle. He stopped midway and turned around to look at her, and the sadness in his eyes wrenched her young heart. What difficulties would this young boy face because she bargained with God? A sudden surge of doubt slipped into Dove's consciousness, and she had to force herself to shut out the boy.

She turned her attention to Reverend Honeycutt. "I guess you won't be needing me here anymore tonight," she said.

"No, Dove," he answered sadly, his voice thick with disappointment. "You can leave now."

Dove put her hand on the minister's arm. Although she had no idea why she was apologizing, she said, "I'm sorry, Reverend."

He patted her hand. "You're a special young lady in God's eyes, Dove. I doubt that He is finished with you." Seeing the look of panic etched on her face, he amended, "Someday He will work through you again, although probably in a different way. When He does, you'll be ready for it." He smiled at her fondly. "But right now I think your mom and dad are anxious to talk to you."

Dove hurried down the aisle. She didn't believe for a minute that God would ask her to do anything ever again.

"How did it go?" Ann asked anxiously.

"Great! Nothing happened, Mom. I didn't feel a thing." But that wasn't completely true. Dove felt a void—an emptiness she couldn't explain.

Ann closed her eyes in a silent prayer of thanks.

Dove quickly turned to Bob. The look in his eyes troubled her. It wasn't exactly sadness or disappointment. It was more like maybe he wished God hadn't wasted His time giving the gift to her, but had given it to him instead. But when he squeezed her hand, all her worries fled. He was still her friend.

Dove took Maddy's arm and they walked ahead, then waited for their parents and Bob to catch up. Out of the corner of her eye, Dove saw the young boy in the church courtyard. As he looked at her, Dove was aware of the question forming in his eyes: *Why didn't you heal me?*

Suddenly, a sadness enveloped her. She didn't fully understand it, but she knew it had something to do with him.

"Maddy, do you know the boy in the wheelchair?"

Maddy followed Dove's gaze and shuddered.

"What's the matter?" Dove asked. "Somebody walk over your grave?"

"You and your superstitions!" Maddy grimaced, rolling her eyes upward.

Dove sighed in exasperation. "It's not a superstition, only a saying. You don't have a grave anyway, silly. So what made you shake all over?"

"I don't know," she said with a nervous tremor in her voice. "I got some kind of premonition . . ."

"Is that different from intuition?"

"Yes, it's like a—a warning."

Before Maddy could explain, Bob caught up to the girls. The three young people joined Ann and Joe at the car and piled in the backseat.

A swell of happiness filled Dove, sitting so close to Bob, and she looked from him to Maddy and then to her parents. What more could she possibly ask for? Everyone she loved was with her. And God had finally listened.

Once again the image of the boy in the wheelchair flashed across her mind and her happiness dimmed. Could she have changed his destiny tonight if . . . ? Darn, she was beginning to think like Maddy. Dove loved her sister, but she wasn't ready to start thinking like her.

Dove suddenly realized that she wasn't freaky anymore. She'd keep her bargain with God and go to church every Sunday, but no one would stare at her and think her weird. That was all behind her. But best of all, she had a boyfriend. A real, live boyfriend. She couldn't wait for school to start so she could tell all her friends about Bob. And she and Bob would go to all the dances and games together. A shiver of excitement ran through her as she envisioned herself in a fancy gown going to the senior prom. Maybe she'd even wear her hair up, Grecian style.

But intertwined with her happy thoughts was the memory of the boy's face as he looked up at her from his wheelchair. Dove shuddered. They had arrived home, and Bob was walking her to the front door.

"Cold?" he asked.

"A little."

He put his arm around her, and something in his eyes told Dove he understood.

"Bob," Dove said softly, "Reverend Honeycutt said the strangest thing to me." She repeated the minister's words that she was special and that God wasn't finished with her yet and would work through her again.

Bob's eyes met hers. "You *are* special, Dove."

True to her word, Dove no longer complained about her red hair or skinny legs. She had her hair cut in a short, sassy style, and as her mother so aptly put it—she was filling out. Maybe she'd never have the soft, sweet look of Maddy, but she had something else. That summer, several of her mother's friends asked her if she'd ever thought about modeling. Dove was flattered by this new attention, but the glamorous life wasn't for her. She was a simple girl with simple tastes. Her Mexican friends called her *simpática*.

The summer sped by, crowded with beach activities during the day, and bowling, movies, and double dates with Maddy and Allen filling the warm evenings.

One night, over ice cream at the Busy Bee, the four young people were discussing their futures. Allen announced he would join the air force after high school and go to college when he finished his stint in the service. Bob planned on becoming a minister when he graduated from college. His family was still very much against it, and Dove was his sounding board.

"After college I'm coming back to Catalina and opening my own snorkeling shop," Dove announced.

Maddy made a face. "Not very glamorous. You really should think about modeling—or maybe studying acting. I always said you were distinctive."

"Oh, Maddy, you know I don't like being in the limelight." She lowered her head and took a sip of Pepsi. "What about you? What glamorous things are you going to do?"

"I have it all planned. I'm going to major in art with business as my minor and open a stained-glass shop right here on Catalina. My pieces will reflect the sea, the beach, the sky." She spread her arms wide to encompass the island. "All of this beauty will be captured in my work. And the tourists will love it and buy everything I make. Then when I'm really good, I'm going to design and make church windows."

"You do have big plans," Allen said in awe.

"And they'll happen. Mark my words."

After the boys dropped them off, Dove asked Maddy if she could talk to her.

"Sure. Are you having problems with Bob?"

"No. Nothing like that. I'll change into my pj's and meet you in your room."

Maddy was sitting on her canopied bed when Dove

arrived. She moved over to make room for Dove. "What's up?"

Dove drew in a long breath and then slowly let it out. "I'm not exactly sure. Ever since that night . . . the night when . . . when I lost . . ."

"The healing?" Maddy prompted gently.

Dove nodded. "Ever since then I keep seeing the boy in the wheelchair. We never did find out who he was, did we? Well, anyway, I have this . . . this empty feeling, like something inside me is dead. Mostly I'm happy—especially because of Bob—but a piece of me seems to be missing. I can't explain it. It's like a big hole or . . . or . . ."

"Void?"

"Yes, void. But worse, I don't even know what it means. . . ."

Maddy took Dove's hand. "I think God wants you to fill that emptiness with something that would honor Him."

"Is He mad at me because of what I did?"

"I don't think so. I just think He wants you to do something for Him and in that way fulfill yourself."

"But what can I do? I don't have any special talents."

"You don't have to have any to work for God. Think about it and pray about it. The answer will come to you."

"Easy for you to say. Answers always come to you."

"But you're the one God wants to work in. Not me," Maddy said softly.

"Oh, Maddy," Dove cried, throwing herself in her sister's arms. "I'm scared."

"Don't be," Maddy soothed. "If this is God's wish for you, He'll help you."

Dove wiped her eyes and studied her sister. She wondered why God had chosen her instead of Maddy—Maddy, who seemed to know all about the way God worked—who could always comfort you no matter how badly you hurt—who was sweet and gentle and kind.

"Thanks, Maddy. You always make everything all right."

As Dove climbed into bed she felt weightless—free and

light. It was a good feeling. She remembered to say her prayers, but fell asleep somewhere in the middle of them.

Three days later, Dove ran into Reverend Honeycutt on Summer Avenue. "Hi, Reverend," she said gaily, raising her hand to shade her eyes from the noonday sun.

"Hello, Dove. Enjoying your summer? You must have spent a lot of time at the beach to get that tan."

Dove smiled. "Are you teasing me, Reverend Honeycutt?"

"No," he laughed. "I know how difficult it is for someone with your coloring to get tan at all. Makes you look healthy."

"Thanks." They started to walk away from each other, but something made Dove turn back. "Reverend Honeycutt?" she called.

"Yes?" he answered, turning around.

"The boy in the wheelchair—who was he?" She hadn't meant to ask about him. It just slipped out.

He cleared his throat. "A visitor from New York. He spent a week on the island with his aunt."

"Oh." She hesitated slightly and then said, "Are there any others around like him—I mean, kids in wheelchairs who might need someone to push them around or play checkers with—or help them with their homework? Never mind; that was a silly question." If there were any such kids, she'd see them at school. She turned away again.

"Dove?" Reverend Honeycutt said, putting his arm on her shoulder. "Don't keep blaming yourself for not being able to heal that boy."

"I'm not. It's just that—oh, I don't know." Dove shifted her weight from one foot to the other. "I feel like I want to do something for others since I didn't help him. He really thought I would, too. I could see it in his eyes. He must hate me—and God."

"On the contrary. His aunt says whenever he writes he asks about you."

"He does?"

Reverend Honeycutt nodded.

"There must be something I can do on this island that would be meaningful."

The minister studied her a moment. "Would you like to help the nurses in the children's ward of the hospital? Sometimes there are more children than the nurses can handle, with all the paperwork they have to do. The kids need to be fed and played with and held. Parents can't always be there. What do you think?"

Dove's face beamed. "They really need someone?"

He nodded.

"Oh, Reverend Honeycutt, I'd love to do it. When can I start?"

"Let me call the hospital and talk to the head nurse and get back to you."

"You won't forget, will you?"

"No, I won't forget."

"Will I be able to do it? I mean, supposing I drop one of the babies or something."

"Don't worry. You'll do fine. I wouldn't have suggested it to you if I wasn't sure you could handle it. Besides, the nurses will give you instructions on how to handle the children."

"Thanks, Reverend. I'll be ready anytime they want me. School starts next week, and my last class is out at two-thirty. I can go right after school."

Dove ran all the way home to tell her mother and Maddy. Ann was excited for her daughter, and they discussed changing their dinner hour on the days Dove was at the hospital so she could stay and help feed the children. Maddy hugged Dove and winked, giving her one of those "I told you so" looks.

When Dove told Bob later that night, he was visibly moved to know she cared enough about sick children to volunteer her time. "How about if I volunteer too. Then I can walk you home. It'll be getting dark early pretty soon."

"What a great idea. We can work together. Why don't

you call Reverend Honeycutt and see if the hospital can use both of us.''

"I'll call tomorrow.''

"You just might turn out to be another Doctor Spock.''

"And you a Florence Nightingale.''

Dove was experiencing an inner joy. Not only because Bob was going to volunteer with her, although that was part of it, but mostly because this was something she was going to do for God and, in return, for herself.

Early the next morning Paloma's loud purring woke Dove, and she lay quietly in bed going over the events of the previous night. It had been the most perfect night of her whole life. Not only had God answered her prayers, but on the way home from their date at the bowling alley, Bob had held her hand. They had held hands before when he'd helped her up from the sand or when she'd grabbed his hand in excitement. But this was different. This was a more grown-up kind of hand-holding. Looking down at her long fingers lying on the pink flowered sheet, she could still feel Bob's touch.

"Paloma, I'm going to wake up that lazy twin sister of mine and make her ride with me to Pebbly Beach before the sun rises.'' As if to answer, the kitten stretched and then curled up into a ball.

Quickly tugging on shorts and a halter, Dove tiptoed down the hall to Maddy's room. "Maddy, are you awake?'' She whispered so she wouldn't disturb her parents.

"What time is it?'' Maddy asked groggily.

Opening the blinds, Dove answered noncommittally: "Early.''

"Then why are you up and dressed?'' Maddy asked, leaning on her elbow.

"I want to ride to Pebbly Beach before the sun comes up.''

"Are you for real? Why in the world do you want to go so early?''

"I don't know. I'm just so excited about yesterday I can't sit still—meeting Reverend Honeycutt accidentally, and then his asking me to help out at the hospital—and Bob holding my hand as if he wanted to keep it forever. I couldn't sleep. I just had to get up and do something. And I don't want to go alone. Come with me," she coaxed, pulling on the sheet. "You can sleep tomorrow."

"Oh, all right," Maddy said hesitantly, hugging her knees to her chest.

"What's bugging you? Don't you want to go?"

"It's not that I don't want to. It's just that I have this feeling that maybe we shouldn't."

"If you're worrying about Mom, we can leave her a note. . . ."

"It's not Mom. I'm getting the same feeling I had that night when I looked at the boy in the wheelchair."

Dove groaned. "That's past, Maddy. All over and done with."

Maddy studied her sister a moment, then cocking her head, she asked, "You're really set on going, aren't you?"

Nodding enthusiastically, Dove answered, "I have all this energy inside me that's ready to burst if I don't let it out."

"Okay, let's do it." Maddy hopped out of bed and grabbed a pair of shorts and a shirt. In the kitchen, she filled a plastic bag with chocolate chip cookies while Dove scribbled a note to their mother and propped it up against the empty cookie jar. The sun had begun to rise, but dark, ominous clouds obscured it.

Dove suggested they take Clemente Street and ride up the mountain road past the Wrigley Mansion and down to Pebbly Beach the back way instead of taking the direct route from Front Street to Pebbly Beach Road.

Once they left Clemente Street, the road was a steady upward climb. Several times they stopped to catch their breath and sat on the roadside, munching cookies while watching the lizards scramble into the bush. Suddenly the sun broke through the clouds, resting on the delicate white tree poppies. The gray-green leaves of St. Catherine's Lace were transformed into shimmering silver.

"Ready?" Dove asked, and Maddy nodded, picking up her bike. When they reached the summit point, they stopped again, this time to look down on the Bay of Avalon. "Isn't it funny," Dove said, "how the boats are all in a row so nice and neat, and yet when you see them from the beach they look like they're anchored just any which way."

"Mom would say, 'It's the perspective.' "

Dove made a face, wondering why Maddy used all those fancy words. "Let's go. It's downhill all the way now. Race you." She mounted her bike and rode off, turning occasionally to make sure Maddy was following.

When they reached Pebbly Beach road, they rode side by side, as there weren't many cars on the road so early in the morning. The sun, still low in the sky, was now out in full force.

Dove was on Maddy's right, shading her eyes with her hand. Suddenly, she saw a car make a wide turn around the curve, a flash of sunlight bouncing off its windshield. The terrible squeal of car brakes shattered the silence, and the car careened toward them. "Maddy!" she shouted, her voice drowned out by the sound of a horrible crunch. A scream tore through her as she watched Maddy's body sail through the air and over the embankment. The crumpled blue bicycle landed in the dirt; chocolate chip cookies dotted the road.

Leaping from her bike, Dove ran to the embankment and stared down at the jagged rocks jutting out of the water. Maddy's limp body lay sprawled, her legs twisted hideously, her long dark hair partially covering her face. The only movement was the swirling dark water slapping against the gray rocks.

"Maddy! Maddy!" Dove screamed, scrambling down the rocks and slipping on their wetness, ignoring the sharp edges that dug into her knees and tore at her fingernails. Fear gripped her insides, and for a split second she thought she was going to be sick. She sucked in her breath to steady herself and then kept her eyes on Maddy during the rest of the climb down.

Why wasn't she moving? Why didn't she answer? This couldn't really be happening. It had to be a nightmare. "Please God, let me wake up," she whispered. Then she was kneeling beside her sister, and when she looked at her broken body she knew it was real.

"Don't touch her," a man's voice called from above. "I'm going to drive into town to get help. Stay with her, but don't try to move her. Do you understand?"

Through tears, Dove looked up at the man. The reflection of the sun shone on his glasses. Then he disappeared.

Wiping the damp hair from Maddy's face, Dove sobbed, "Oh, Maddy, don't die. Please don't die. I'm sorry I made you go with me. We should've listened to your premonition." She wiped her arm across her wet face. "If I hadn't talked you into going, you'd be home sleeping now." Trying not to look at Maddy's twisted and broken legs, Dove touched the ashen face, her heart about to break.

"I promise I'll never again ask you to do something you don't want to do, if you'll only open your eyes and tell me you're okay. Please, Maddy. Please." Dove buried her face in her hands. She prayed, begging God to save her sister. How long she knelt there, she didn't know. It seemed a lifetime. Then she opened her eyes to see if her prayers had been answered. But there was no movement on the rock except the breeze playing with Maddy's long black hair. Dove sat there, shocked by the deathly white features. Sudden outrage surfaced as she stared at her twin lying immobile. "You can't die, Maddy. You hear me? You can't!" Dove screamed hysterically, over and over.

Suddenly, she heard scramblings, and Doctor Morrison, their longtime family physician, knelt beside her. His fingers touched the inert body.

"You go up and wait while I examine your sister," he ordered.

Dove shook her head. "I'm not leaving Maddy."

"Listen, Dove. Your parents are on the way. The man

who hit Maddy described the two of you when he ran into my office for help. Right after we rang for the ambulance, we called your dad. They'll be here any minute. Now, do what I say and wait for them on the side of the road. I need to attend to Maddy."

Dove climbed up the rocks, her legs so rubbery she could hardly make it. She crawled over the embankment just as her mother and father drove up.

Ann opened the car door and looked around frantically. Spotting Dove, she ran to her. Joe was right behind.

"Mom. Dad. Maddy's hurt. She's down there on a rock," Dove cried out as she threw herself in her father's arms. "Oh, Dad, she's not moving. I tried to talk to her, but she won't answer." Joe moved Dove to his side and kept his arm around her protectively, even as he peered down on the rocks.

"Oh, dear God," Ann cried in a strangled voice and started to climb down.

"Doctor Morrison says we're to—to stay—up here," Dove said, stammering in fear. But Ann merely threw her an impatient glance and would have gone had Joe not grabbed her arm. At the same moment, they heard the shrieking of the ambulance siren. An attendant jumped down and told them to wait where they were, explaining they'd only be in the way.

Mother, father, and sister huddled together, watching the two attendants pull out the stretcher and scramble down the rocks. When Dove looked up and saw her father crying, she completely lost control and began screaming, "It's all my fault. I should be the one down there. Not Maddy. She doesn't deserve to be hurt. I do. Oh, God, let me change places with her. Please," she sobbed and fell to her knees.

Joe gently helped Dove to her feet and wrapped her in his arms. "It's nobody's fault. It was an accident. Don't you know I'd feel just as bad if you were lying down there?" Dove bit her lip so hard she could taste the blood.

Ann walked over, and the three of them clung to each other.

When Maddy was secured on the stretcher, she was cautiously carried up. They moved toward her, but were only able to catch a fleeting glimpse as she was lifted into the ambulance. Ann was stunned by Maddy's waxen face, and a shiver of fear ran through her.

"She's dead, isn't she?" Dove screamed. "And it's all my fault. I made her go. She didn't want to," she sobbed, "but I made her. I killed her, Mom. I killed her." Her voice rose in hysterics.

Joe shook her sternly. "Please try to calm yourself. You didn't make her go, Dove. She went with you because she wanted to. I must talk to the doctor. . . ."

Dove crumpled against her mother, still sobbing.

Dr. Morrison stopped in front of them. "She's alive," he said gravely and put his hand on Joe's shoulder. "I'm afraid she's in very serious condition, however. We have to get her into surgery right away. Meet me at the hospital." He jumped into his car and drove off.

Ann put her arm around Dove as they walked to the car. Some of the initial shock was wearing off, and the words Dove had been pouring out began to register on Ann. "No matter what happens to Maddy, you're not to blame. Do you understand? It was an accident." Dove's eyes were glazed with fear and emptiness; Ann doubted that she had even heard her.

But Dove had heard every word. You're wrong, Mom, she answered silently, while desperately wanting to believe her mother. It *was* all my fault that she was out there where she could be hit. No matter what anyone said, she knew that whatever happened to Maddy was because of her.

When they reached the car, Dove looked at the cookies scattered in the road and she felt as if she were going to suffocate.

She got in the car and sat between her parents, staring straight ahead as her father drove to the hospital. She replayed the horrible scene of the accident over and over in her mind, seeing Maddy's body hurtling down, landing on the rocks.

Ann could sense Dove's self-incriminating thoughts. She knew she had to pull herself together so she could help her. But thoughts of Maddy's inert body besieged her, and it was difficult to concentrate on words that would comfort Dove. Ann needed comforting herself—and so did Joe. And Maddy. What did Maddy need? Was she even alive?

Ann didn't think she'd be able to cope with the death of one of her children. If Maddy died, how would they go on? How would they survive without her gentle presence? And dear God, how would Dove survive her feelings of guilt?

Before her mind had a chance to sort out the answers, Joe pulled the car into the hospital parking lot. They ran toward the entrance. When Joe asked about Maddy, the desk nurse told him she was being prepared for surgery and they were waiting for his signature before beginning. After he signed the forms with shaking hands, the young woman suggested they have a seat in the small waiting area.

"Want some coffee, hon?" Joe asked Ann after a while.

She looked at him uncomprehendingly, then slowly nodded. "Thanks. Coffee would help."

He dropped some coins into the machine and handed a cup of black coffee to Ann. After getting some for himself, he slipped some money into the soda machine. He pulled a cold bottle of Pepsi out of a slot and handed it to Dove, his fingers trembling. But Dove merely held it. Nothing would pass the awful lump that was choking her.

For the first half hour they sat huddled, talking in whispers. Suddenly Joe stood up and paced the small waiting area. Ann pulled Dove over to her side and held her close, but Dove sat stiffly, unable to yield to the comfort of her mother's arms. Each time there was movement near the nurses' station, their heads turned expectantly. When the nurse shook her head, they would numbly turn back to what little comfort they could find in each other.

Ann felt Dove's body, rigid next to hers, and she sensed Dove was bottling up her emotions. Joe continued to pace back and forth, running his fingers through his hair, his face tense with worry. We have to get it out in the open, Ann thought.

"Dove? Can you talk about what happened?"

Eyes numb with shock, Dove merely nodded.

"I think it might be a good idea if we did," Joe said, sitting down beside her, elbows on his knees.

Dove stared at the floor. Finally, in a monotone, she dragged the words out. "I—I was so happy this morning—had to get out—do something—I asked—no, I talked Maddy into going. She didn't want to go." A shudder ran through her. "She said—said she had a—a premonition—like the one she had at church. . . ." Her voice trailed off and she swallowed convulsively.

"Premonition? At church?" Joe asked.

"When she saw the boy in the wheelchair." Dove droned on, still not looking at anyone. "She got chills and—and shook all over. She got that same feeling this morning. That's when she told me a premonition was like a warning." Hot tears boiled over and Dove doubled over, her face in her hands. "I should've listened to her," she sobbed through her fingers. "We never should have gone." Then her head jerked up, and she stared angrily at them, as though all this was somebody else's fault. "If she had this premonition, why didn't she just say no? Why did she let me talk her into going?"

Ann patted her arm, desperately trying to calm her. "You know how Maddy is. It's almost impossible for her to say no to someone, especially you, Dove. She'd rather die than disappoint someone she loves."

And that just might happen, Dove said silently.

"Were you riding against the flow of traffic?" Joe asked.

Again, Dove waited before answering, as though it took

a while for the question to register in her anguished mind. "No. We were on the right side."

"Then how did the car hit Maddy?"

Dove gave a deep, shuddering sigh. "I don't know. I had to put my hand up—sun in my eyes. A car came around the curve. Sun on his windshield—like fire. The car turned wide—came toward us. Maddy was on the outside. I screamed for her to get out of the way." Dove began to tremble. "Something hit and then Maddy came—oh, Dad, she came flying up in the air—over the embankment." She began sobbing and put her hands up to her face. "Everything so fast—yet—yet like slow motion."

Dropping her hands to her lap, she began twisting the hem of her shorts. "I screamed and screamed—climbing down the rocks—she just lay there—not moving—legs twisted. I wanted to—to make her move. That man told me not to touch her." Her eyes glazed. "And I couldn't do anything to help her. Nothing. Nothing. Nothing," she cried out, pounding her thighs with her fists.

Suddenly, Dove crumpled into her mother's arms, their tears mingling. "Tell me she won't die, Mom. Please. Tell me she'll get better."

"I wish I could, Dove." She smoothed Dove's hair from her face. She wished she could give comfort to this poor distraught child, but right now she needed comfort herself. Turning to Joe, she said, "Would you ask the nurse where the chapel is? I need to do something more constructive than worrying. I need to pray."

The nurse motioned to a room down the hall. "Dove? Are you coming?" Joe asked as he took Ann's hand and helped her up.

"You go. I'll wait," she answered dully.

Ann nodded. "Okay. Come and get us if Doctor Morrison comes out."

What in the world was taking the doctor so long? Dove wondered. It seemed as if she'd been waiting for days, but of course it really was only a couple of hours. Still, nobody had given them any news about Maddy. That probably meant she was still alive. Dear God, please let her be alive, she prayed.

Her knees were cut and scraped from the sharp rocks and encrusted with blood and her fingernails were broken, but she was only vaguely aware of it all. Her heart was in that room behind closed doors—in there where Maddy was lying. Then she heard a sound, and Doctor Morrison was standing before her.

"Maddy?" she asked fearfully.

He touched her cheek. "She's holding her own. Our surgeon, Doctor Ward, is still working on her, but he should be finished shortly." He looked around the small room. "Where're your parents?"

"They're in the chapel. I'll go get them." She started to rise.

"No, don't bother them right now," he said, placing a hand on her arm. "You can tell them what I told you when they come out. I'll see them when Doctor Ward is done. I'll know more then." He returned to the operating room.

Dove looked up to see Bob walking toward her, relief in his eyes.

"Dove, are you okay? I just heard about the accident and came right to the hospital. Where're your parents? Where's Maddy?" Out of breath, he threw himself in the chair next to her.

Grabbing his hand, Dove sobbed, "Oh, Bob, you're here. I'm so glad. Mom and Dad are in the chapel." Then she bit down on her bottom lip to keep from bursting into tears. "Maddy's in there." She jerked her head toward the operating room door. "She's been in there a long time. But Doctor Morrison just told me she'll be out pretty soon. I'm so scared, Bob." She ended in a whimper and buried her face in his shoulder.

"What happened?" he asked, putting his arm around Dove and patting her back gently.

Dove repeated the story. She felt completely drained when she'd finished.

"Should we go into the chapel?" Bob suggested.

"No. Someone should be here in case Doctor Morrison comes back. But if you'll wait out here, I'll go tell my mom and dad what he said when he came out earlier."

"Okay. I'll stay." His eyes were filled with compassion.

A few minutes later, Dove returned and sat down next to Bob. His presence and the pressure of his hand on hers gave her strength. She knew he was there to help her through this crisis, just like her dad was there for her mom. Suddenly, she found herself talking about Maddy and their childhood—remembering the things they did together. It was as though talking of the past would hold back the awful present.

Then right in the middle of telling about a prank Dove tried to talk Maddy into playing on one of their teachers, her voice broke and she sobbed, "Bob, do you think God will take her from us?"

He shook his head, but Dove saw tears form in his eyes.

"What'll I do if He does?"

Bob squeezed her hand. "He won't. She's going to be okay. You must keep believing that."

She looked up into his deep blue eyes, searching for assurance, and saw something that brought a measure of calm. Faith—that's what it was. Faith, like Maddy always had. And it was something she needed right now. Holding tight to Bob's hand, she felt some of his trust in God's goodness flow into her.

When Ann and Joe returned from the chapel, Dove noticed that they, too, seemed calmer, though her mother's eyes were still red-rimmed from crying.

"Bob, how nice of you to come," Ann said softly, hugging him when he rose to greet her.

"I came as soon as I heard. I'm sorry about Maddy, Mrs. Sanders."

The noise of footsteps intruded. Doctor Morrison headed toward them, fatigue showing in his eyes. He pulled up a chair and sat facing all of them as they sank down anxiously onto chairs against the wall.

"Maddy's in stable condition," he said without preamble. "She has internal injuries, but Doctor Ward was able to correct them."

Dove breathed a sigh of relief that quickly changed to fear when she saw the look in Doctor Morrison's eyes. He's not finished telling us, she thought.

Doctor Morrison looked down, as though he couldn't face all their beseeching eyes. Taking Ann's hand, he said, "I'm so sorry—I wish I didn't have to say this, but Maddy suffered damage to her spinal cord when she landed on the rock."

Dove gave a little moan that was echoed by Ann. Doctor Morrison looked up, his own eyes wet. "She's paralyzed from the waist down."

I must not have heard him right, Ann thought. He couldn't have meant Maddy—not my sweet, lovable Maddy, never to walk again? She saw Dove from the corner of her eye and turned to see her tortured face.

"No—no, you're wrong!" Dove heard herself screaming. She wanted to beat on him, force him to change those awful words. Maddy wasn't crippled. She couldn't be. Not her Maddy. How long she screamed her outrage at the doctor she didn't know, but even as her father gathered her in his arms, she heard the doctor speak again. "Of course, you'll want to take her to a specialist on the mainland when she's able to travel. . . ."

A steely numbness overcame Dove. What would a simple village doctor know about spinal problems? Dad would get specialists, doctors who could fix Maddy. She'd be okay. But the fear that Doctor Morrison might be right strangled her hopes. Vaguely, she heard him say something about a tranquilizer for herself and Ann, and for the first time Dove was aware of her mother.

Ann's face was white and drawn, her eyes glazed, and she was trembling. Joe tried desperately to hold on to Dove and comfort his wife. Even Bob seemed stricken. Though Dove saw their grief, she felt apart from it. They don't ache like I do, she thought dully. It's not their fault Maddy's hurt.

Doctor Morrison turned his attention to Dove's taut face. Rising to his feet, he bent down and brushed a tear from her cheek. "I wish I could tell you it wasn't true, Dove, but I can't. Maddy's very badly hurt, and she's going to need a lot of help in the weeks and months to come. She's going to need you especially."

Dove stared through him, as if she hadn't comprehended a word he'd said. But she had. She understood very well. And all she wanted to do was die so the hurt would go away.

Chapter Nine

Doctor Morrison had told the family to go home and return later when Maddy regained consciousness, and now they sat in the living room. Ann and Joe spoke in short broken sentences, but Dove had not said anything since her hysterical outburst at the hospital. Bob sat beside her, holding her hand, but she felt nothing—not even gratitude. No, that wasn't true. She felt an immense emptiness—an emptiness that only Maddy's presence could fill.

Vaguely, she wondered why Allen hadn't come. Surely he'd know by now. It seemed everyone on the island knew. The phone was ringing when they walked in, and finally her dad had to tell the callers to hang up—that he was waiting for word from the hospital.

Dove kept remembering the boy in the wheelchair and Maddy's shuddering reaction. Had she seen herself that way?

Unable to bear being around the others, knowing she was responsible for Maddy's condition, Dove slipped quietly upstairs—one of the few times she didn't take the stairs two at a time. In her lethargy, she even forgot to say good night to Bob.

"I must get back home," Bob said quietly to Joe when Dove's door closed upstairs. "Tell Dove I'll see her later."

He touched Ann's lowered head. "And please tell Maddy I'll be praying for her."

Ann nodded and mumbled her thanks. Joe glanced at his stricken wife, then walked to the front door. He followed Bob outside.

Ann rose and walked into the kitchen, and her gaze fell on the rack of mugs hanging over the sink. ANN, JOE, DOVE and MADONNA, she read silently from left to right. She reached for Maddy's mug and held it reverently, looking at the letters that made up her name. Dear, sweet Maddy. What will her life be like if she can't walk? Ann placed the mug on the table and dropped her head into her hands. Deep sobs racked her body.

After yielding to her grief, she brushed away the tears. She had always been strong, and now wasn't the time to weaken. Her family needed her—not only Maddy, but Joe and Dove. She understood their need to be alone and was wise enough to give them space. If she gave them time, they'd rally together as a family. And that's what counts right now—that they band together—not only for Maddy's sake, but for their own.

Though she doubted anyone would eat, Ann began fixing a light meal.

"Ann," Joe called through the screen door, "come sit outside for a while."

Placing the cold roast chicken back in the refrigerator, she joined her husband on the porch, sitting down next to him on the top step.

"I'm sorry I walked out on you, but I had to get myself together." Joe put his arm around her.

Leaning into his shoulder, Ann said, "I understand. We all need some time alone." She took a deep breath. "You know, Joe, it's almost as if we expect this horrible accident to go away if we don't acknowledge it. That once we talk about it, it'll become a reality. The sad part is that whether we talk about it or not, it's real. There was an accident. And Maddy's in the hospital." She hesitated over her next words, speaking them softly: "And I'm afraid will spend the rest of her life in a wheelchair."

Touching his face gently, she continued: "Those are the facts, Joe, whether we remain silent or not."

He shook his head. "Two months ago we didn't have a care in the world. And look at us now."

Ann stared straight ahead. "You realize of course that it's not just Maddy we have to deal with. It's Dove, too."

"I know. She's beating herself with guilt."

Ann took his hand and held it tightly. They sat silently for several more minutes until she said, "Come on. Let's go in."

Joe followed her into the kitchen. "Don't you think we should call Dove down?"

"Let's give her a few more minutes while I fix us something to eat."

The doorbell rang shrilly and Joe went to answer it. Ann blanched when she saw Doctor Morrison enter the kitchen.

"Maddy's still holding her own," he quickly assured her. "I came by to see how all of you were doing, to see if there was anything you needed. I didn't have much time earlier. . . ."

Ann thanked him for his concern and questioned him about the extent of Maddy's internal injuries and the damage to her spinal cord. Was there any possible hope that her daughter might walk again?

The doctor shook his head. "It's just as I told you at the hospital. The most we can hope for is that the rest of her will heal properly. But truthfully I can see no hope for her legs—short of a miracle, that is."

Involuntarily, an image of Dove's hands came to Ann's mind. That's between Dove and God, she reminded herself.

After asking about Dove and telling them they could now visit Maddy for a few minutes, Doctor Morrison left for his hospital rounds. He promised to call if there was any change in Maddy during the night.

Ann climbed the steps to Dove's room. Knocking on the

door lightly, she went in. Dove was sitting on the bed brushing Paloma, her head bent over the kitten.

When she looked up, Ann noticed her red and swollen eyes. She sat down on the bed next to Dove, and told her of Doctor Morrison's visit. "Would you like to go with your dad and me to see Maddy?"

A flicker of fear touched Dove's face. "Not yet, Mom. I can't. Not yet."

"That's okay. You don't have to go today. Maybe you'll feel up to going tomorrow." Ann took Dove's hand. "Will you be all right by yourself? We won't be any longer than a half hour."

"I'll be fine. I'll stay here in my room."

Ann smoothed Dove's russet hair and bent over to kiss the top of her head and started to leave.

"Mom?"

"Yes, honey?" She turned at the door to face Dove.

"Tell Maddy I love her and that I'm sorry."

Swallowing a large lump, Ann answered, "I'm sure she already knows how you feel. . . ."

"Tell her anyway, Mom. Please." Dove's blue eyes swam in tears, and Ann felt her own eyes fill up again.

"Okay, honey. I'll tell her." She closed the door softly behind her.

Dove listened as her parents prepared to return to the hospital. Only after she heard the car drive away did she move from the balcony door. She ignored Paloma, who stretched luxuriously and seemed to want to be scratched. Instead, she knelt beside her bed, hands tightly folded, her eyes pleading as she gazed out the open balcony door to the blue sky beyond.

"God, can You hear me?" she asked, her voice thick with unshed tears. "I need to ask You something. Please don't get mad at me for being off-again, on-again, but this is really important. I have to have the gift of healing back again—just this once. Please God—just one more time. I won't ever ask You again to change Your mind. I promise. But I desperately need the gift right now. It's my fault

Maddy's legs are paralyzed. I have to do something to help her. I can't let her sit in a wheelchair for the rest of her life. You understand, don't You, God?''

She remained kneeling, her eyes closed now, as she waited for God's answer. But none came. All she heard was Paloma's loud purring nearby. Finally her knees began to hurt and she got up. She looked at the kitten and then sat down beside her on the carpet.

"How silly of me," she told Paloma, pulling her close. "God doesn't *talk* like we do. He answers prayers by *doing* things—like He didn't *tell* me the gift was gone. It just was."

She felt better. God had heard her prayers before; He would hear them again.

When her parents returned, she hurried downstairs. "How's Maddy?"

"Still groggy from the anesthesia," Ann said, and Dove noticed that her eyes were still red from crying. "I don't think she knew we were there. But I gave her your message." Tears puddled in her eyes and she turned away.

Dove looked at her father. "She's not dying, is she?" she gasped.

Joe folded her in his arms. "No, honey, she's going to live. She's got a sturdy constitution. The nurses and doctors say she's progressing well. But she's still only semiconscious. Just as well you didn't go. She'll be wide awake by tomorrow." He hugged her and kissed her red hair. "It takes more than an accident to keep our Maddy down," he added. But to Dove his voice didn't ring true.

They walked into the kitchen, which was always the favorite talking place, but when they sat around the table, Maddy's empty chair screamed at them.

They spoke quite calmly about Maddy's prognosis, then Ann added, "Dove, please don't blame yourself for what happened. . . ."

"But I *begged* her to go when she didn't want. . . ."

Joe cut in. "Maddy had the power to say no. It was her decision to go. If she *really* felt the premonition of danger, she could have refused to ride with you. Don't take on the burden of guilt. . . ."

Dove didn't hear the rest. Suddenly, she realized what she must do. Helping at the children's ward wasn't the way to fill the emptiness inside her. She had to get the gift back and heal Maddy.

After her parents went to bed, Dove opened her bedroom door quietly and looked toward their room before stepping out of her own. She waited several seconds. Hearing only silence, she tiptoed down the stairs, hoping they wouldn't creak and wake her parents. When she made it safely down, she carefully opened the front door. She walked softly until she reached the corner, then broke into a run for the hospital.

Mrs. Larson, the night nurse, glanced up to see Dove standing at her station. "Dove, what are you doing out so late?"

"Please. I have to see my sister. It's very important." She shifted her weight from one leg to the other.

Mrs. Larson looked at her kindly. "Visiting hours were over long ago." She picked up a clipboard. "And it says here on your sister's chart that visitors are only allowed for a few minutes at a time."

"I just want to see her for a few minutes," Dove pleaded. "I won't wake her, I promise. I just need to see that she's all right. Please, Mrs. Larson, she's my twin. I can't go to sleep until I see her—just for a minute," she whispered, touching the nurse's sleeve.

Mrs. Larson smiled gently. "I understand, honey. There's no one here right now, so I think it'll be all right if you just slip in—only a few minutes, though." Pointing down the hallway she said, "Room 108."

Dove stopped in front of Maddy's door. Then, taking a deep breath, she slowly opened it and tiptoed to the bed. She was barely able to make out her sister's face in the darkened room. When her eyes adjusted to the dim light and she saw the tubes attached to Maddy, a shiver ran through her. Despite that, Maddy seemed to be sleeping peacefully, and Dove watched the sheet rise with each breath she took. Then she remembered why she was there, and her gaze traveled down the length of the sheet.

Laying her hands on Maddy's legs, Dove closed her eyes, willing heat into her hands. Nothing happened. "Please God," she whispered. "Please." Staring at her hands, she concentrated on the light, airy feeling she remembered experiencing with Mrs. Farley. But still nothing happened. "You can punish me, God, but please don't punish Maddy. She didn't do anything."

"Dove?" Maddy whispered hoarsely.

"Oh, Maddy, I wasn't supposed to wake you up. I'm sorry." She needn't have worried; Maddy had fallen back into a deep sleep.

Closing her eyes, Dove said, "I'm going to try one more time, God." For the second time, she placed her hands on Maddy's legs, trying to recapture the feeling she'd had in church. She squeezed her eyes closed and softly sang the Lord's Prayer. Still no heat—no peaceful glow. Nothing. The gift was gone. And God wasn't giving it back.

Choking back sobs, she whispered good night to Maddy, then left the room, barely remembering to thank Mrs. Larson. She walked home in the dark, the weight of her grief slowing her steps.

The house was still when Dove tiptoed up the stairs into the safety of her room. Utterly dejected, she turned on the small bedside light and sat down on the bed. "He didn't give it back to me," she said aloud, tears trickling down her face. "He didn't give it back." Suddenly she became angry. "I don't know why. If He can do anything like everyone says—then what's the big deal? I sure had Him pegged all wrong."

Disgusted with herself and God's lack of interest, she quickly undressed and climbed into bed, only to toss and flail about for hours. Finally, when she realized she wasn't able to fall asleep, she climbed out of bed and turned on the small bedside lamp and looked around for the Bible. She wasn't going to give up. God had answered her before this way—maybe He'd answer her again.

Dove closed her eyes and let the Bible open at random. She lifted her gaze and read from Ecclesiastes: "For everything there is a season and a time for every matter under Heaven."

She stared at the page dumbly. What in the world did that have to do with anything? Frustrated, she dropped the Bible on the night table and climbed back into bed. It was almost daylight before she finally fell asleep.

The next morning, after a breakfast nobody ate, the Sanders family walked to the hospital. Dove didn't mention that she had visited Maddy the night before. And unless Mrs. Larson was there and said something, Dove didn't intend to bring it up. What was the point? She had tried and failed. Nobody needed to know that—not Bob, not her parents, nobody. Only God. And He didn't seem to care.

Doctor Morrison was at the nurses' station and greeted the Sanders with news that Maddy was awake and had been told about the accident. "So far," the doctor said, "she's taking everything quite well."

"You haven't told her about her legs yet, have you?" Ann asked.

"Not yet. She knows she has no feeling in them, but she thinks it's temporary. We'll see how she does today and then perhaps tomorrow. . . ."

"Please be sure we're here with her, doctor," Joe said.

"Of course," Doctor Morrison answered.

Upon entering the room, Ann noticed that some of the tubes had been removed from Maddy. However, the I.V. was still dripping slowly. Maddy's pale face was framed with her long dark hair, but she looked a little better than she had yesterday afternoon.

"Mom, Dad, Dove," she said weakly. "I'm a mess, aren't I?"

Moving quickly to her side, Ann took her daughter's

hand and then bent down to kiss her. "You're alive, Maddy. That's all that matters. The sooner you can come home, the better."

Joe stood beside Ann and smoothed back Maddy's hair. "How are you feeling, sweetheart? Are you in pain?"

"A little. Mostly I'm just tired." Turning her head, she looked at Dove. "Were you here last night, or was I delirious?"

Dove shrugged, trying to look nonchalant. "Must've been delirious. Visitors aren't allowed at night."

Maddy looked from Dove's hands down to her own legs. "I guess so," she said.

A few minutes later, the day nurse poked her head in. "Time's up. Doctor Morrison left orders that visits were to be limited to five minutes each today. You can come back this afternoon at two."

Ann and Joe caressed Maddy's face, telling her they'd be back in the afternoon, and started for the door. Dove lagged behind, and Ann turned to her and said, "Just one more minute, Dove, then you have to leave."

"Okay, Mom. I won't stay longer than a minute."

With eyes half closed, Maddy said, "You were here last night, weren't you? Why?"

Dove shrugged away her question. Taking a deep, fortifying breath, she blurted out: "Maddy, do you hate me?" She wasn't sure what she'd do if Maddy said yes.

Maddy's eyes widened in surprise. "Why would I hate you?"

"For what happened to you. It was all my fault." Dove turned away and looked out the window, afraid of Maddy's answer.

"Don't be so silly. The accident wasn't your fault," Maddy said, then her voice grew weaker. "I could never hate you. No matter what. Remember that," she said, her eyes closing.

"But you don't know," Dove whispered, looking down at her hands.

"Know?" Maddy mumbled. "I only know I could never hate you. Never."

Through tears, Dove looked thankfully at her sister, but she was fast asleep.

Maddy seemed to have a little more strength in the afternoon, but she still tired quickly. When their five minutes was up, Dove left with her parents.

That night, at eleven, Dove once again left her house undetected and walked to the hospital. She hoped Mrs. Larson was on duty.

She was. "Back to see your sister?" she asked as though aware that this girl needed time alone with her twin.

Dove nodded.

"You were so careful last night I don't see any reason not to let you visit her again tonight. Try not to wake her, though. She needs her sleep."

"Thanks," Dove whispered and walked down the hall. She entered Maddy's room and tiptoed to the bed, feeling for Maddy's legs in the darkened room. Then she carefully pulled up a chair, and sitting on its edge, put her hands on the sheet and began singing the Lord's Prayer in a voice slightly more than a whisper. She concentrated hard on the meaning of the words. Everything had to be just right.

When she finished, she shook her head as she looked down at her uncooperative hands.

"Dove, are you trying to heal me?" Maddy asked softly. "What is it? What's wrong with me?"

Dove remained silent, hoping Maddy would fall asleep again. Beads of perspiration trickled down her back.

"You must tell me. What needs to be healed?" Maddy's voice grew louder, bordering on panic.

"I wasn't supposed to wake you. I'll get Mrs. Larson in trouble," she hedged.

Maddy lay back. Her brown eyes locked with Dove's. "It's my legs, isn't it? I have no feeling in them. They said it was temporary, but it isn't, is it?"

Dove stared at Maddy, not knowing what to say.

"Dove, answer me," Maddy insisted. "I have a right to know."

Pushing the chair away, Dove fell on her knees next to Maddy's bed. "Yes, yes. I tried to heal you. But I can't," she cried out in total despair. "I asked God to give me back the gift, but He didn't listen. It's all my fault. Everything is my fault. I want to die, Maddy. I want to die," she sobbed, her head on the sheets.

"My legs are paralyzed, aren't they?" Maddy persisted in her soft voice.

Dove nodded, unable to look up at her sister. When the silence dragged on, she raised her head. Maddy's face was turned away. She hates me, was all Dove could think.

"I'm sorry, Maddy," Dove whispered. "I'd give anything to be able to change places with you. Anything," she murmured, her voice breaking. "Only please don't hate me."

Finally, Maddy turned back to her sister, her face unnaturally calm. "It's not your fault. It's not anyone's fault. It's just some—some terrible thing that happened." But her dark eyes, illumined with tears, held the unasked question—Why?

Dove shook her head slowly, her thoughts far away. "Why . . . why didn't God listen to me, Maddy?" The words of anguish were torn from her throat.

"I don't know," Maddy answered in a voice still numb with shock.

"But I could have healed you."

A heart-wrenching sadness crept into Maddy's voice. "You don't know that for sure."

"But suppose . . ."

"The gift is gone, Dove." Maddy raised her hand to silence her twin and then stared at the ceiling, a look of agony on her beautiful face.

Dove's feeling of guilt made her continue, without giving much thought to her words. "Don't you see? You're going to have to spend the rest of your life in a wheelchair. Because of me everything is—is hopeless."

Maddy winced, but spoke calmly. "Nothing is hopeless. With faith, miracles can—and do—happen." She closed her eyes, and for a moment Dove thought she'd drifted off into sleep.

Suddenly, Maddy's armor cracked and she began to sob. "What am I going to do without my legs?" she cried out, clutching at Dove. "How will I get around?" Reaching out with both hands, Maddy cried in desperation, "I'm afraid, Dove. Oh God, I'm afraid." With an unexplained strength, she pulled Dove closer and wrapped her in her arms. "You're going to have to help me," she sobbed. "You're going to have to be my legs." She buried her head in Dove's shoulder. "Promise me."

Dove hugged Maddy's head close to her and choked back the sobs that lodged in her throat. "Oh, I will, Maddy, I will. I'll do anything you want. I swear."

"Don't leave me tonight, Dove. Please don't leave me here all alone," Maddy pleaded.

"I'll never leave you."

Their tears mingling, Dove and Maddy clung to each other until Mrs. Larson separated them, just before dawn.

Chapter Ten

From the window Dove saw Maddy. A band tightened around her heart as she watched her sister deftly maneuver the wheelchair, just as she had for the past twenty-two years.

The pool gate swung closed as Donna leaped from the pool and ran over to her aunt, giving her a bear hug. Maddy didn't seem to notice the water dripping on her dress as she squeezed Donna tightly around the waist. Laughing, Maddy handed Donna a small box wrapped in blue and white paper.

Then Dove watched as Maddy reached over the side of the wheelchair, picked up something small and white from a basket, and handed it to Donna.

Shrieking her excitement, Donna raced into the house, clutching the white furry bundle.

"Mom, Dad, look! Aunt Maddy gave me a kitten for my birthday. And it's all white." She ran into the dining room and dropped the small box on the table with her other unopened presents, then came back into the kitchen, holding up the kitten for her parents' inspection. Her father was sitting at the table slicing tomatoes.

Dove turned from the window and walked toward Donna. "What a precious kitten. Is it a girl?" she asked just as she had so many years ago.

Donna nodded. "Aunt Maddy said it was. Didn't she give you a white kitten once for your birthday?"

Dove nodded, tucking her hair behind her ears. She glanced at Bob before answering. "It was *our* fifteenth birthday. Paloma was very special to me."

"Can you actually remember way back to when you were fifteen?" Donna teased.

Dove and Bob both laughed. "It wasn't all that long ago!" she said.

Yes, Dove remembered. That was the day her life began to change. Nothing was ever the same after that—especially not Dove.

She grew up quickly after Maddy's accident. Her faith and trust in God came back slowly—yet more firmly. She learned to let go—let God—not to fight and beg and plead, but to accept. And look how wonderful her life had turned out. Bob was a loving husband and Donna and Robby the joys of her life. And to complete her happiness, her parents and Maddy were living nearby. God had been very good to her.

Donna, standing by the window, broke into Dove's thoughts. "Look, Doctor Franklin's here with the kids from the Deaf and Blind School." She turned from the window and put her arm around her mother. "You've been working with these kids for a long time now, haven't you? Is it frustrating, Mom? I mean, either they can't hear or can't see. Sometimes neither. How do you communicate with them?"

"By touching—and loving—the way God communicates with us. He touches our lives and He loves us even if we reject Him. Even though I turned away from Him once, He never stopped loving me. Look how I've been blessed," Dove said softly as if speaking to herself. She felt Bob's eyes on her.

"I can't believe *you* ever turned away from God!" Donna said.

"I know. It's hard for me to believe, too," Dove said in a whisper. Bob rose from the table and walked over to her.

"How did you . . . ?" Donna persisted.

Dove took Donna's face in her hands. "Not now, Donna. But someday I promise I'll tell you all about it. It's not something I usually talk about." Bob placed his hand on Dove's shoulder and squeezed it gently.

"Sure, Mom." Donna tried to read the expression in her mother's eyes. She looked at her father. He had that same look.

In an effort to lighten the mood, Bob said, "Have you decided on a name yet for your kitten?"

Dove glanced down at the white ball of fur and took it from Donna, holding the tiny animal up to her face. The kitten had light blue eyes. She reminded Dove of Paloma.

"I'm not sure," Donna said. "I kind of like Snowflake. That way if she grows up to be a neat cat I can call her Snow for short, and if she turns out strange I can call her Flakey."

Dove laughed and ruffled her daughter's damp chestnut hair. "Assuming she's going to be a neat cat, why don't you take Snow to your room. She'll get trampled on outside—or worse, she'll get lost."

As Donna took the kitten from her mother and began walking through the dining room, Bob called out, "There's cold soda in the cooler at the side of the house and punch in the fridge. Check first with Doctor Franklin before giving any to the school kids. And on your way out, would you pick up the veggies and dip for your guests to nibble on before I start the hamburgers?"

"Okay," Donna called back.

Bob kissed Dove on the cheek. "I think I'll get the grill fired up." The screen door slammed behind him.

Looking over at the small box wrapped in the blue and white shiny paper lying on the dining room table, Dove wondered what was inside. An image of gold seashell earrings flashed across her mind. She quickly shook off the momentary feeling of *déjà vu* that assailed her.

Donna's arms were laden with picnic food; she asked her mother to open the door for her. Dove stood in the doorway, watching Donna move from group to group offering refreshments. The yard was quickly filling up with teenagers. Bob was emptying a bag of charcoal. Robby snuggled against Maddy and then suddenly climbed off her lap and toddled over to the sandbox.

Dove returned to the dining room and picked up the small box Maddy had given Donna. She turned it over, memories tugging at her.

Not only had Maddy never complained after the accident, but she'd managed to hold on to an air of expectancy throughout the years—as if a miracle might happen to her at any time. Faith and hope shone from her eyes. And she constantly talked about the power of believing. So much so, that over the years she'd continued physical therapy on her legs even though the doctors told her repeatedly it was useless. Maddy didn't want her legs to atrophy. Some day, she said, she was going to walk again.

Shaking her head in amazement at her sister's unwavering faith, Dove returned to the kitchen and finished icing the cake. She ran the bowl under water while savoring the remaining chocolate left on the spatula. Then she went out to join the party.

"Let's play some games with the kids before we eat, Mom," Donna suggested. "You sign to the deaf and I'll gather up the blind kids. When we get everyone together, we'll hold hands and make a big circle of love."

Donna rounded up the sightless children, and coaxed all her friends, even Doctor Franklin and Maddy, into the circle.

"She has such a way with people," Bob whispered to Dove.

"And so much love for everyone."

"I wonder who she takes after," Bob said, looking at Dove with affection.

"Okay, everyone. First, 'London Bridge is falling down.' " Turning to her mother Donna said, "Sign to the kids, Mom."

Five minutes later, after recovering from the laughing,

giggling, and falling down, Donna said, "Next we'll do 'go in and out my window.' Ready, Mom?"

Dove signed.

As they began, Bob said, "I think I'm too old for this.'

Dove playfully nudged him in the side. She looked around at the children's glowing faces as Donna helped them put their hands together to make the windows for the others to walk through.

There was a lot of tripping and stumbling, but they finished amid squeals of merriment. "Okay, everyone," Donna said, out of breath. "One more and then we've all earned our hamburgers." The group cheered. "This time we'll do ring-around-a-rosy."

Wiping grass from their shorts, the children stood up and grabbed the nearest hand. Dove was between Robby and Bob. Donna was directly across—a blind girl on either side of her.

> Ring around a rosy,
> A pocket full of posie,
> Ashes, ashes, we all fall down.

On her hands and knees, Dove looked up to see Donna and one of the blind girls, Isabelle, still standing. They were turned toward each other, immobile, like statues. The younger girl was clutching Donna's hand and staring into her eyes.

Suddenly everything seemed dreamlike. Aware of an aura around Donna, Dove rose to her feet. It was at that moment that she realized Isabelle's eyes were no longer vacant—unseeing. She felt lightheaded.

In a daze, Dove walked over to them and reached out to her daughter. An unexpected tremor swept through Dove as her hand touched Donna's and she felt the searing heat flow from her daughter's hand into her own.

Seemingly unaware of her mother's presence, Donna's lips moved silently as if whispering prayers that only God could hear.

Isabelle, oblivious to everyone except Donna, traced the contours of Donna's face with her free hand. A tear rolled down the young girl's cheek. "Praise the Lord," she whispered. "I can see!" She fell to her knees in thanksgiving, while the others looked on in astonishment.

Warmth continued to flow from Donna's hand to Dove's as mother and daughter stood motionless. Bob swiftly moved to Dove's side, and Donna released her mother's hand.

In awe, they watched Donna kneel next to Isabelle. Then, smiling, she took Isabelle's hands and raised her to her feet.

Bob held on to Dove as she swayed under the emotional strain. "This is a long-ago prophecy coming true," he said.

Dove looked at him, perplexed.

He tightened his grip on her. "Remember what Reverend Honeycutt told you?"

Suddenly Dove heard the minister's words as clearly as when she had stood in front of him in the Little Church on the Hill on Catalina Island: *"You're a special young lady in God's eyes, Dove. I doubt that He is finished with you. Someday He will work through you again. . . ."*

Dove turned to Maddy. Something in the depths of her sister's tranquil eyes said this was what she had been waiting for so patiently. And Dove knew then that God *was* working through her. The gift of healing had been passed from mother to daughter. And Donna had accepted the blessing.

Speaking with only their eyes, Dove and Maddy both knew that God had given them a second chance.